# JOURNEY

by

D.W. Lewis

The Caerwyn Chronicles
Book I

**Author's Note:**
This series is set in a historical period in which slavery, violence, and social injustice were tragically common. These elements are depicted for the sake of historical authenticity and storytelling, not as an endorsement of such practices.
The author does not condone slavery or oppression in any form. Where these themes appear, they are meant to illuminate the human cost of injustice and the enduring struggle for dignity, freedom, and compassion.

This series stands firmly with those who resisted, endured, and sought freedom in the face of injustice.

**ISBN:** 9781972803004
**Renaissance Hands Books**
2nd Edition

# Part I

# The Journey Begins
# (45 AD)

# Chapter 1

The sun was coming up, and the ground was slowly warming as Corin walked through the mist rising from the grass. Corin pulled his wool cloak tighter across his chest, the weather was getting warmer as they came to the summer months but this morning there was still a chill in the air. He had lived for fourteen summers and loved the warm air the summer brought. The sheep that Corin were herding were happy to be able to eat the new green grass that was starting to show life again after the cold winter.

They came to a small valley between two hills where a creek would give them water to drink. Corin liked bringing his sheep here to let them graze and he could sit under one of the trees and dream. As the sheep moved around him, Corin settled in his favorite spot and put his staff beside him. He had been bringing the herd here for years now and they knew to stay close. Corin sat and looked out across the valley, careful to watch for any dangers, but knowing there would be few in this field.

As the sun rose into the sky, Corin opened his cloak to allow the sun to warm his skin. As he was starting to doze in the sun he saw movement across the valley. He rose quickly and grabbed his staff, looking to see if there was a threat. He realized it was a person. As the person got closer, he recognized the awkward gait of Eira. She had grown taller recently and walked like she wasn't used to her long legs.

He had known Eira as long as he could remember, her family and his were neighbors and she was only a year younger than he was. She had brown hair , brown eyes and big teeth. She was the youngest of three girls and her clothes never seemed to fit as she always wore her sister's old clothes. Corin sighed and laid down his staff. Eira was annoying, but she was no threat.

"Corin!" Eira called to him, "my father wanted me to find you. I looked everywhere, but here you are." Corin rolled his eyes, of course he was here. He was always with the sheep.

"What does he want?" Corin asked, irritated.

"Bran is hurt," Eira said as she walked up to Corin. Bran was Eira's brother. He kept sheep as well, so he and Corin often helped each other. Bran was smaller than Corin, most people were smaller than Corin who was tall for his age. He often enjoyed an afternoon working with Bran, keeping their sheep together on large fields. "Father is hoping he can bring the sheep to join yours for a few days."

"Let him know where I am," Corin said. "I'll watch them." Eira let out a large breath as she sat down next to Corin. She was obviously out of breath from her hurried search. She needed to catch her breath before returning to her father.

"It's warm today," Eira said, unfastening the brooch that held her cloak on. She removed the cloak and laid it next to her. She was wearing a plain brown tunic underneath and her dark brown hair fell in a loose plait down her back. Corin looked at her and suddenly realized that she was starting to look more like a woman. The tunic fell in a way that revealed curves that he never thought of her having.

"Are you going to tell him?" Corin asked.

"Yes," Eira responded, "when I'm ready." She glared at Corin. When they were younger, Corin had been a good friend. They often played together, but as he got older, he preferred to spend time with her sisters. Eira's mother had told her this was how all boys were. She still liked Corin, she liked his hair that never seemed to sit still on his head and found his quick smile charming.

Corin leaned back against the tree and stared out at the sheep. He could feel Eira watching him, she was always staring whenever they were together. He glanced at her and wondered if she would ever grow into her ears, they stuck out on either side of her head. He realized how mean the thought was and chastised himself. She was not unattractive; her small nose crinkled every time she spoke which was cute.

"I should go find father," Eira said, standing up again. "He wants to get the sheep to you soon so he can do what he needs to do." Eira turned and smiled at Corin, like she was expecting him to say something.

"Right," Corin said, "I'll wait here." Eira grabbed her cloak and rushed off. Corin stood up and walked around, counting the sheep to make sure none had wandered off. They were all still close to him, so he walked back to his tree and sat down. He spent some time imagining he was a warrior, fighting for the honor of his family. His father had been a warrior when he was a younger man. Corin imagined he could do the same.

Sometimes he would bring a bow out here and practice his aim. His father had promised to give him a spear when he could kill a rabbit at a distance of ten paces. He was almost able to manage that with a still target, rabbits were harder to get close to, so he was working by sneaking up on the sheep.

The sun was high when Eira's father, Bronac, brought his own sheep into the valley. Corin walked to him as soon as he saw him coming. He lowered his head with respect and greeted Bronac.

"Eira tells me she spoke with you," Bronac said. He was older than Corin's father, Eira's mother was his second wife after his first had died. His grey hair was long and laid across his shoulder like a cloak. He had a crooked nose and square jaw. Corin had learned as he got older that Bronac was a good man would do almost anything for his children.

"How is Bran?" Corin asked.

"He fell while fixing the roof," Bronac said, the thatched roofs of their roundhouses often needed small repairs done. "He hurt his side and cannot breathe well. I will keep him close to me until he is better."

"I will bring your sheep home tonight," Corin said, Corin had done it before, and Bran had done it for him when he gashed his foot open on a rock and couldn't walk for a week.

"You are close to manhood," Bronac said. It was often around the fifteenth or sixteenth summer that a young boy would be considered a man. Corin stood a little taller and smiled. "Tell your father I wish to speak to him." With that Bronac walked off leaving Corin wondering what Bronac wanted to speak with his father about.

The evening came soon enough and Corin took the sheep back to his roundhouse. As he was separating them, he mentioned to his father that Bronac wanted to see him. Corin's father was still a strong man with broad shoulders and a big chest. He nodded and suggested they go together with the sheep. The walk took some time and Corbin's father walked in silence.

When they arrived, Corin led the sheep to the pen while Bronac and his father walked off to talk. Corin decided to take the time to see how Bran was and walked over to the roundhouse. He called out to announce himself and Bran's mother Briganti came to the entrance to invite him in. The hearth in the middle of the house was glowing with bright red embers giving some light in the dark room. Bran had a bed close to the door and was resting there. Corin went to him and put a hand on his friend's shoulder.

"How are you feeling?" Corin asked. Bran had dark brown hair, the same as Corin. In fact, these two looked like they could be brothers, similar hair and build, both tall and powerfully built. Corin had lost some of his childish facial features, while Bran looked like a boy in a man's body. Corin's square jaw and straight nose made Bran jealous that he didn't look as handsome as his friend.

"I felt something inside me snap," Bran said. "It will take some time to heal I think." Corin sat on the floor by the bed and told him about the day with the sheep, what they ate and where they went. As they were talking about where he should take them tomorrow, Eira walked over from the hearth with a dish of bread and potage, a stew made from lentils.

"Hello Corin," Eira said, "I didn't see you come in."

"Hello Eira," Corin said. Eira looked around the house, as if looking for something.

"Did your father come?" Eira asked.

"He did," Corin said, and this made Eira blush a little. Corin had seen her blush a few times, usually when embarrassed. She wasn't embarrassed easily, but when she was, she turned a bright red.

Eira sat down next to Corin and stared at him again. Bran let out a low chuckle and Eira glared at him. There was something going on that Corin didn't know about. He was about to discover what as his father came into the house with Branoc.

"Son," his father said to him, "Branoc and I have discussed it, and we have decided that you are to marry Eira." Corin felt the air rush out of him. Eira had been a friend, they had grown up together. She wasn't a woman to marry, she was a girl that annoyed her. He looked at her; her smile went from one ear to the other.

"Thank you!" Eira said, jumping up and embracing her father. Corin stood and watched the excitement in Eira's behavior. He didn't want to hurt her by saying what he was thinking.

"Thank you, father," Corin said. He was now promised to Eira. It was a moment he had been looking forward to, learning who he would marry. He didn't think it would happen like this. He still had several years before they would join in marriage. He would be expected to reach manhood first, and Eira was not yet a woman. Looking at her now, almost exploding with excitement, she seemed to still be a little girl.

with his head covered in a hood. In the glow of the firelight his face was in shadow. He pulled back his hood and Corin saw he had a scar on his cheek that was still red. He looked around the crowd, taking in a deep breath he started.

"My name is Talan," the man said, "I fought alongside my brothers to protect Iscalen. When the iron army came, we could hear them in the distance. The armor they wear is loud, it can strike fear into you." Some of the men in Corin's village wore metal armor, but most men had thick leather armor. "They are organized and come in a line," Talan continued, "all you see are their shields and they approach."

"Were you able to break the line?" a deep voice called out.

"A few of us managed to get our spears past the shields," Talan continued, "but when one man fell another took his place." There was some muttering among the men. Corin's heard his father asking a man close to him what they could do against a force like this.

Corin was a little confused, he thought the men always knew what to do. Whenever trouble came, they would gather and come back with a way to solve the problem. He looked around the group and could see they were all very worried. Corin wondered if the elders were really that much different than he was after all. He felt some concern about the idea that the men were not much smarter than he was. He turned to his father.

"Is it always this way?" Corin whispered.

"What way?" his father asked.

"Nobody knows that to do," Corin said.

"That is why we meet," his father responded, "we decide together what to do. It is important that we are all have worked together." Corin shook his head and turned back to the men.

"We should run," one of the elders was saying, "find a place to hide in the hills." This seemed reasonable to Corin. His father stood and put a hand on Corin's shoulder.

"We should fight!" Corin heard his father say. "Me and my son will stand for Caerith. This is our home. My father and his father are buried here. I will not abandon them." Corin's father had taken him to the burial mound where his ancestors were buried. He told him about his grandfathers and what they had done. Corin could almost feel their presence that day, they had overcome great difficulty to get this land safe and free.

There was a loud cheer from many of the men, but others seemed less convinced. Corin wanted to hide, but he would not go against his father. He believed with his whole being that his father was right. If you fight for your land, you remain free, if you cower and hide you lose.

One of the eldest men in the group, bent from the weight of his years stood up. The crowd went silent as he walked over to the fire and, using his walking stick, poked at the wood to make the blaze burn brighter. The flames danced beneath his white beard, and he stood as tall as he could.

"We fight for Caerith," he said in a hoarse voice, "we fight for our own freedom." He looked at Corin, who was the youngest in the group. "We fight for our families and keep our land free for our children." He turned and walked back to the circle and the group remained silent. When the old man rejoined the circle, there was a loud cry of assent, they would fight.

The ale was brought out and passed among the men. They drank and told stories of past battles. Things that had happened before Corin's time. Battles that had kept the land free for him to be able to care for the sheep and wander the hills. This went on late into the night. The ale made Corin tired and he curled up into a ball by his father and slept. There was something comforting about being a part of such a powerful group of warriors.

# Chapter 3

The mist was thick in the valley below where Corin stood with his father and the other warriors from the village. It had been two cycles of the moon since the night they decided to fight and news had come that a group of the iron men were coming through the valley. The elders had sent this group of men to stop them. They had scouts watching for the enemy but so far there was no news.

Corin rested his shield on the ground and let it lean against his body. He had been given leather armor and a sword. His father had taught him to use the shield and sword to fight but he was nervous that he would forget everything he learned. During practice it all seemed so simple, but now he was unsure of himself. Standing here among the trees and waiting for men that had killed many people, Corin felt real fear for the first time in his life.

A man came rushing up the hill from the valley and said something to one of the men at the edge of the woods. Corin heard a spear beating against a shield. The sound echoed through the valley. This was the signal to prepare for battle. All the men started to beat their shield, the sound getting louder as they joined in. Corin hit his shield with his spear as well, he could feel the energy growing as the sound grew. A rhythm developed as they all joined together. They were strong, they would win!

The sun was cutting through the fog, and Corin saw a glimpse of the men coming into the valley. They were wearing shiny armor and metal helmets. They carried shields that were painted red and had a golden bull painted on them. They all wore red tunics under their armor. They were identical, each man looked like the other.

Corin's father grabbed his arm and pulled him over to where a wagon with two wheels was being loaded with spears. Two men were taking position, one at the reins to control the horse and the other on the side with his shield up against the rail on the side. As he was not familiar with fighting with swords, Corin was to ride on the wagon and use the spears to attack. There was a railing on the side of the war-cart for him to hold on to, but other than his shield, there was no other protection. There were five of these war-carts preparing to ride to the back of the line of iron men and attack from the rear.

"Corin," his father was saying, "look for red cloth, thrust your spear into red cloth." Corin felt the fear coming back but stepped into the wagon, taking a spear.

"Red cloth," he said, firming that into his thoughts. The wagon started moving and Corin almost lost his balance. He reset his footing took a deep breath, balancing his shield the way he had been shown. The wagon moved fast and he could feel a breeze passing through his hair.

As they rode through the woods, the trees flying by, Corin let his mind go back to Eira. The last few days as he had been preparing to fight he had no time to see her. She came to visit him last night. She had handed him a small pouch with a leather strap he could wear around his neck. Inside the pouch was a lock of her hair.

"Keep this with you," she said, looking deep into his eyes. Corin had slipped it over his head and let the pouch fall against his chest. He could feel that it would protect him and was wearing it now. As they stood there, he had looked at her lips, he had never thought of kissing her before, but at that moment had wanted to. She smiled and her small nose wrinkled, did she know what he was thinking?

The driver of the wagon was calling back that they were coming up to the enemy. They were still among the trees and the three men let out a battle cry, the other war-wagons were doing the same. Corin could see the iron men at the back of the line turning to look at them as they came upon the group. They turned too late as the first war-wagon came upon them and spears were thrust into the men. Two of them fell and another ran into the woods.

As his wagon came among the men Corin waited until he saw a flash of red, he thrust his spear and felt it land on flesh. He pushed harder and lost grip as the spear was wrenched from his hand by the speed of the wagon. He picked up another spear and prepared himself, watching for more red. He thrust again and felt the spear hit something solid. He let out a curse and reset the spear. The driver of the war wagon looked his way for a moment and laughed at the language.

"You are a true warrior!" the driver said and he pulled the reins to avoid a fallen tree. The wagon turned too quickly, and the wagon went onto one wheel. Corin lost his balance, falling from the wagon. It righted itself and drove off without him. Corin grabbed for his sword and pulled it awkwardly from its sheath.

Corin saw one of the iron men standing close by. He was wearing a helmet and iron armor but had apparently lost his shield. Corin saw his own shield on the ground and picked it up, putting it in front of himself he rushed at the iron man. There was a loud clang, and he felt the man give way a little before he started to push back. Corin tried to thrust his sword around his shield the way he had been taught, but it caught on the edge of the shield and was moved away from his body. He felt the shield vibrate as a sword connected with it.

Corin pushed again, and the shield twisted to the side. He saw a flash of red and without thinking thrust his sword into it. He felt resistance as it came against flesh. Corin pushed with all his might and heard a guttural scream from the other side of the shield. The weight against the shield fell off and Corin looked to see the man lying on the ground. He couldn't know if the man was dead or alive, but he was no longer a threat, so Corin turned to move on.

As Corin turned, he saw a flash of light. He turned in time to avoid the sword that had been coming for his head. He moved his shield toward the man coming at him and pushed into his new enemy. There was a loud crash as his shield connected with the other man's shield. He thrust his sword around the shield blindly and his arm was jarred as it jammed into something hard.

Corin put all his weight behind his shield and pushed again, knocking the other man backwards. As he shifted his weight, he could feel the pouch from Eira tucked beneath his armor. He suddenly knew deep inside he was protected and would win this fight. He put all his strength into a push against the shield and felt the man on the other side push back, but Corin managed a step. He was pushing this man backwards!

Another push and the man lost his footing and fell backwards, Corin tumbling on top of him. He felt the air rush out of his opponent moved so he was face to face with the man. He was not much older than he Corin. Corin could see the fear in the other man's face but was so filled with the rage of fighting he jumped to his feet and thrust his sword into the spot of flesh he could see beneath the man's helmet. Corin could tell he had killed this man. He looked around to see if anyone had noticed, but everyone was fighting hard for survival.

Corin's arm was sore and tired, but he lifted his shield once more. He took his sword out of the dead man's neck and ran towards the fighting. He saw his father fighting one of the iron men, they had both lost their shields and were fighting sword to sword. Blood was coming down his father's face and Corin was afraid for his father. He ran towards the men and jammed his sword into the other man's side.

Injured, the man jumped to face his new opponent. Corin saw the flash of his father's sword and the iron man fell dead at his feet. Corin let out a loud cheer and his father looked at him. Corin could see pride on his father's face, it was a warrior's dream come true; father and son defeating a common enemy.

The iron men were running away into the woods. There were a few that had been taken captive, but most of them were dead. Corin was filled with a burst of energy, and he chased some of the iron men into the woods. He moved quickly, but it wasn't long before he couldn't see them anymore. All his strength was gone and Corin sat down on a rock for a moment to catch his breath.

A moment later an old friend, Doran, who was a few seasons older than he came running by. Doran stopped and sat next to Corin on the rock. Both were quiet as they realized it was over and they had both survived. Corin looked at his sword, the tip was still red with the blood of the man he had killed.

"I killed three," Doran finally said. Smiling at Corin.

"I killed two for sure," Corin responded, "maybe three." Doran stood and put out a hand to Corin.

"We will be expected to help gather the dead," Doran said. Corin took his friend's hand and stood. They walked solemnly back to where the men were already moving among the fallen. They were picking up the bodies of those killed by the iron men and placing them carefully by the hillside. A wagon would be brought to take them to the burial mound.

Corin and Doran carried one man to the side, being careful to collect his spear to be buried with him. It was important he had it for the afterlife. Everyone was moving quietly and with respect for the fallen. There were a few men who were wounded who were escorted or carried off to the village where the women waited to care for them.

After the dead were collected, they moved among the fallen iron men to collect weapons and armor. Corin saw his father and walked over to him. He had dried blood on his face from a small wound on his forehead. His father beckoned him over. Corin joined him as he looked at the fallen enemies.

"You did well son," his father said, "you are a true warrior." Corin's chest filled with pride at hearing this. "We must make a sacrifice to Camulos." Corin nodded solemnly, Camulos was the god who protected warriors and gave them victory. The man that drove the war-cart came over to them carrying a broken spear.

"Your first kill," the driver said, handing Corin the broken spear. The tip was dark with blood.

"This is what I will give to Camulos," Corin said quietly. His father gave him an encouraging nod.

# Chapter 4

The men were returning; word had come that they had won the battle and would be coming home. Eira waited by the great hall in the village waiting for news of her Corin. She had been in love with him since she was a little girl. They had been friends for as long as she could remember, but she remembered back to the day she fell in love.

They had been playing by the creek when some boys came and pushed her in, laughing as she came out drenched. Corin had seen this and punched the boy that pushed her. He then fought the other two boys who had been laughing. He was bigger than most boys his age and won the fight easily. He then walked home with her and made sure her mother knew that the mud-covered clothes were not her fault. He was her hero and she never forgot that. When her father started talking about who she should marry she begged him to arrange for her to marry Corin.

When her father had seen that Corin was always willing to help when needed, he had decided that would be a good arrangement. He needed to convince Corin's father, but as the families had been neighbors for many seasons that wasn't too difficult. Now they were betrothed. She felt like she had won a victory.

Today he was returning as a warrior. News had come with the wounded men that they had defeated the iron men. Eira had not seen Corin among the wounded, which was encouraging. She had given him a piece of herself to carry, which she hoped would please Camulos. She knew men often died in battle, but she knew her man would be safe.

People were gathering at the hall with food to prepare a great feast to celebrate the victory. Eira put herself to use by turning the hogs hung over the fire. She had two of them to watch and she kept them turning so they would cook evenly. The fires were hot and kept flaring up as fat dripped from the jog onto the coals. She was sweating by the time word came that the men were arriving. She felt she should clean herself before finding Corin but did not want to wait.

A victorious group of men walked through the gate into the village. Eira watched as the men walked past, laughing and clapping each other on the back. Corin would be at the end of the line, as the least important man in the group. He stood a little taller than most men, so she found him easily. His father was walking with him, the two were talking.

Corin looked over and saw Eira watching and as the group broke up for men to find their families, he came to her instead of going to his mother. Eira's heart leapt as he walked towards her. She knew it was proper for him to come to her first, as his betrothed but she still felt honored. Her hero back from battle.

"Eira," Corin said, "we won a great victory!" Eira clapped and almost put an arm around his neck but stopped herself. They were not married yet and any sign of affection was watched carefully. She contented herself with walking by his side as they went to the long house where the feast would be held.

"I'm glad you're safe," Eira said, looking up at Corin. His face was dirty and he smelled of sweat and blood. He was perfect in her eyes. Unsure what to say, Eira blurted out "We are preparing the feast!" Corin gave her an amused look, and nodded his head.

The men walked into the hall and Corin and Eira followed closely behind. In past feasts, Eira had been expected to serve the food, but now she was promised, and could sit with Corin at the table. She sat between him and his father. Her father had been too old to join the fight but had stayed to defend the village if they had failed. He sat across from them and smiled when he saw his daughter sitting with her warrior.

At the head of the table an elder stood and announced that the celebration should begin. Ale was passed around and soon the roast boar came. There was bread, cheese and some potage available. The feast was amazing and Eira enjoyed the variety of food.

As the evening went on, Corin reached over and carefully grabbed Eira's hand. She felt like her entire body was alert as he touched her. His face was flush with all the ale and heavy food, and he smiled at her.

"Eira," Corin said, "I want to thank you for the charm you gave me, I felt it protected me."

"I'm glad it brought you back to me," Eira said. Corin looked across at her father and called out to him.

"I'm going to give my promised a kiss," Corin announced to Branoc. Branoc lifted his cup and laughed.

"Be careful," Branoc said, "you may be a warrior, but I am still stronger than you!" Eira was a little embarrassed as this exchange. Of course she had wanted to kiss Corin, but having her father watching felt awkward. Corin put his hand gently on her cheek and carefully turned her head. He leaned in and kissed her softly on the lips. It was a short kiss, anything else wouldn't be proper, but Eira felt every part of her singing. It was perfect. His lips were soft and warm. He tasted a little like ale and roast meat. As Corin leaned back in his chair the couple was greeted with a hearty cheer. Eira could feel the blood coming to her cheek, she hated that she blushed so easily.

Any annoyance she had with Corin left when he then leaned towards her and whispered, "I'm glad your father chose me." It wasn't a very deep compliment, but it endeared her to him. Of course, her father hadn't chosen him, she had.

The feast went late into the night, and the sun was almost back to the horizon when they all went to their homes to sleep. Eira stumbled to her bed exhausted but kept thinking back to that kiss. She felt like she had also won a battle tonight, she was certain that Corin would always be hers. She finally managed to get to sleep and slept until the sun was high. She would be expected back at the great hall to help clean. She put her cloak on and walked outside, surprised to see Corin waiting for her.

"I thought I would walk you to the great hall," Corin said. "We will be burying the dead today, so I need to go to the village as well." Eira thanked him and the two started toward the village. As they walked, Corin told her about the battle. Eira wondered what these iron men wanted with them. They seemed barbaric to just come into a land that they didn't know to take land from people. This land had belonged to her people as far back as anyone could know.

"How is your father?" Eira asked after Corin was don't sharing his exploits, "I saw he was as hurt yesterday."

"He's going to be fine," Corin said. "It was a small scratch; he says anything on the head bleeds a lot."

"That is what my mother says," Eira said a little awkwardly. They walked on and Eira felt the silence a little uncomfortable. It was odd, before they were promised she could talk about everything. Now she couldn't think of anything to talk about.

"Do you remember the time we were lost in the forest?" Corin said suddenly. Eira thought back, of course she remembered. They had lost their way and took a long time to find their homes.

"Yes," Eira said, "I was so worried, but you got us home."

"Then you remember it wrong," Corin said with a laugh.

"What do you mean?" Eira asked incredulously.

"You got us home," Corin said. He stopped walking and took Eira's hand. "You gave me directions that you remembered. I didn't believe you at first, but you remembered the path we took." Eira let go of Corin's hand and started walking again. She didn't remember it that way at all. What she remembered was holding his hand and talking about the trees and flowers they had seen on the way.

"I forgot about that," Eira said. "I guess I've always been good at finding my way."

"I was thinking about that last night," Corin said, "I think we are good together. I wasn't sure at first you know." Eira glared at Corin. "I mean it," Corin continued, "I wasn't sure about marrying you. But I now know why our fathers agreed it would be good."

"I suppose we should trust the wisdom of our parents," Eira said softly. It hurt that he admitted he wasn't sure about their being perfect for each other, she had known it for so long.

"Yes, we should," Corin said. "I think our fathers did do the smart thing." Eira walked ahead, smiling.

# Chapter 5

Word had come that a more iron men were coming towards the village. The elders decided it would be wise to move everyone to the village and set up a guard around the village for their protection. The village had a series of deep ditches and a wooden wall for protection. This was the defense that had worked for generations. Most of the people from outside the village were now living in the great hall, knowing they would be protected. It was tight and uncomfortable, but it was the only wise move. They had done it before and would do it again; it was always the way.

Corin set up his blanket on the ground outside the hall for himself to sleep on. As a single man it was thought best for him to stay separate from the women. There were a few men with him, it was always hot inside the hall and the men sleeping outside preferred to be in the cool air. The villagers all ate together, keeping food stockpiled against a siege. They were prepared for the worse.

One morning the iron men appeared out of the forest. Corin took a watchful position on one of the mounds by a ditch, his spear at the ready. They kept coming, there were more of them than Corin could count. They dug their own ditches and built their own walls. They quickly set up huts made of cloth and built cook fires. It was their own village. A village of warriors.

As they were setting up, the elders met and discussed a plan for attack. Corin was not a part of those meetings and was happy he didn't have to decide what to do. He was told to stand guard at the gate. He watched his enemy and fear came into him again. Doran came along a ditch and climbed up to stand with him.

"I'm here to relieve you," Doran said, "there is food at the hall." Corin thanked his friend and started off towards the hall. He had to walk down into the ditch and follow it along until he got to the place he could climb up to the gate. Down here, where he couldn't see the village of warriors, he felt more secure. He was hungry so he moved swiftly to where he could join his family at the great hall.

He realized as he was walking that his idea of family was changing. It used to mean just his mother, father and older sister, now it included Eira. He laughed at himself, he used to want to get away whenever he saw Eira, now he longed to see her. He climbed up to the gate and walked to the great hall. Eira was sitting at the entrance to the great hall, Corin noticed that even with her hair down, part of her ears jutted out. She saw him coming and her face lit up, she smiled and her small nose wrinkled. Corin came and sat with her.

"This is not going to be an easy battle," Corin said quietly to Eira. He felt like a hardened warrior now, who knew everything about combat.

"I trust you will win," Eira said, "I know you are strong."

"There are many of them;" Corin said, shaking his head.

"Toutatis will protect us," Eira said with confidence. They had sacrificed one of the captured iron men to the god who protected the village. When the warrior village was being built, some of the older warriors took one of the captives and hung him upside down in front of the gate. When he started crying out for help, they lowered him into a barrel of ale and kept him there until he died. Surely Toutatis would be pleased, and the enemy would learn what happened to anyone that came against them.

"He will," Corin said. He trusted the gods to protect them, but that wasn't enough for the fear to leave his stomach. Corin looked at Eira, the earnestness in her eyes did help him feel more confident. She trusted him to protect her and the village. She put her hand in his, and looked into his eyes, he looked down at her hand in his. She was so small, he wanted to protect her.

"Corin?" one of the elders walked over to them and looked down at the couple sitting on the bench. "Your father says you are good with a bow."

"Yes," Corin said, "I am."

"We are planning to use arrows against the iron men," the elder said. "The survivors of previous attacks say they stand shield to shield, leaving no space to put a spear. We are going to shoot arrows high over their shields. If Camulos directs them we should weaken their defenses." Corin nodded, this was a good plan.

"I will get a bow and be ready," Corin said. The elder put a reassuring hand on Corin's shoulder then walked off to find someone else to help set up a defense. Eira's expression was one of pride, her man had been given an important role in defending the village. Corin looked away for a moment, staring at the ground. The fear he had felt the last time was coming back, he could feel it deep inside of him.

"I'm thinking we should build our house between my father and yours," Corin finally said, trying to think of a positive future and not the possibility of death. Corin would be expected to start building the house after winter was over. He would need to cut and place the support columns and then Eira and their mothers would help weave the willow branches among the stakes to make the walls. After the mud was placed in the branches, they would light the fire in the hearth and celebrate with a meal together. Once the house was finished, they could plan their marriage.

"I like that," Eira said, "I want to be close to my mother."

"It will be wonderful," Corin said, putting his hand on Eira's hand. As he gazed into her brown eyes, he heard a blast from the carnyx, the battle horn. He jumped up, the men were running to the gate. Word spread quickly, the iron men were gathering for attack.

Corin rushed to where his father was staying in the great hall. There, among his father's belongings, was the bow. Corin grabbed it and rushed to the gate. As he arrived at the gate, there was a man handing out arrows, he handed some to Corin and told him to run across the top of the hill against the wall to get to a position where he could shoot into the enemy.

Corin ran until he had a good view of the enemy. Another man with a bow was standing in the same spot. The iron men had made a line where the shields were touching. Corin put an arrow on the string of his bow and waited for a command to shoot. Soon he heard an elder yelling to release the arrows. He shot high into the air, judging the angle so the arrow should land behind the shields.

Many arrows went into the air and Corin watched them fall into the iron man line. Some did not travel far enough and landed on the ground or embedded themselves into the shields. Corin watched in awe as the line broke and some of them lifted their shields up and they moved together in unison to close the gaps. This gave them protection from the arrows. Only a few made it through to no effect. Corin looked to the men around him each one seemed surprised to see the plan fail.

The iron men were still coming forward, and they had no idea what to do next. The carnyx sounded again and the men scrambled back to the gate. As soon as they were inside, they closed the gate and put a huge beam across it to lock it. Within minutes the iron men were pounding in the gate.

Men rushed to the top of the wall with their spears, thrusting them down at their attackers. But a group of them had their shields held high to protect the men who were battering the gate. Corin rushed to find Eira, she was standing by one of the houses weeping. Corin put his arms around her and fell into his arms, her warm tears falling down his neck.

"We're all going to die!" Eira wailed. Corin wanted to assure her, but he wasn't too sure himself. The well thought of plan had fallen apart in a matter of minutes.

# Chapter 6

The sound of the constant battering of the gate became rhythmic. Corin and Eira stood there for a moment waiting for the inevitable crash as the gate collapsed. Corin had an idea, he whispered to Eira to follow him and then went to the place by the great hall where he had placed his armor. In the rush to get his father's bow, he had left it laying on the ground.  Putting it on, he took up his shield and told Eira to follow him. They went to the wall, close to where the gate stood and waited.

The noise was deafening and they could see the other warriors of the village gathering to defend the entrance. Corin turned to Eira and put his hands on her shoulders. He wanted to make sure she understood what he was going to tell her.

"Stay close to the gate," Corin said, "if we are overrun wait until you see the last of the iron men come in and then run through the gates and don't stop until you reach the woods."

"What about you?" Eira asked.

"Don't worry about me," Corin said, "I will fight."

"What about my mother?" Eira asked. Corin looked at the ground between their feet, trying to think. He looked up and all he could see in her eyes was fear.

"I'll find her," Corin said, "bring her to you. Promise me you will run, if I'm not back with her in time. I will do what I can to get her to you."  Corin was worried she wouldn't leave without her mother so he turned back before she could speak and ran to look for her.

As he was nearing the great hall he saw Eira's mother looking panicked. He grabbed her arm and led her over to where Eira was standing. Mother and daughter embraced. Corin grabbed Eira's hand and turned her to him.

"Remember, when they all come in, run for the woods!" Corin said loudly. Eira nodded slowly. Corin put his arm around Eira, being careful not to smash her with his shield and kissed her. Eira looked up at him, tears leaving streaks in the dust on her face.

"Come back to me," Eira said.

"I will," Corin said. The pounding was getting louder, and they could hear the wood start to splinter. Corin let go of Eira and joined the men waiting by the gate. He put his shield in front of himself and drew his sword. The wood splintered as the gate flew apart, and the iron men rushed through the opening. To get through the opening, they could not make their line of shields, Corin felt they had a chance to fight.

Corin saw a man stumble as he came through the gate, and he rushed the man knocking him down with his shield. The man fell back and Corin came down with his sword. It connected with the helmet and Corin felt a shockwave go up his arm. Corin dug his knee into the man's stomach and felt him struggle to get away. He thrust the sword down beside his knee and heard the man cry out before the man stopped struggling.

Corin stayed in that spot and thrust his sword at some more men. He was rewarded with another cry of pain, and watched the man turn to face him. The man's face was twisted in rage and Corin shoved his shield up to block the sword that was swinging down on him. His left arm was jarred as the sword fell onto his shield. He realized he could see the man's feet and thrust his sword again. The man stepped backwards as his feet were cut open by the sharp edge of the blade.

Corin stood and used his shield to push the man backward. The iron man fell, his head connecting with a rock. He did not get up again and Corin turned to face the next man. As he did, he saw that one of the iron men had found Eira and her mother. He had grabbed Eira and her mother was hitting him with a club. The man cut Eira's mother down with his sword, and Corin heard Eira's scream.

Corin rushed towards Eira, her scream still echoing in his ear. He put up his shield and ran into the man, pinning him against the wall. He let go of Eira as the air flew out of him. Corin dug in deep with his feet and pushed again, feeling the resistance of the man and the wall. He wanted to crush the man but realized with that armor on the man was not going to be crushed.

Corin stepped back and the iron man staggered forward. Corin thrust so hard with his sword into the spot under the man's armor that it went through the man and pinned him to the wall. He was still alive and started clawing at the sword. Corin released the sword hilt and grabbed Eira's hand to lead her away from the village.

They reached the opening of the gate and Corin climbed over the wreck of the gate, indicating to Eira to follow. Eira took one last look at her mother, lying there her blood soaking into the soil. Corin climbed back and put his hands on either side of Eira's face and looked into her eyes.

"She's gone," Corin said, "she died protecting you. Come with me and we will come back and give her a real burial later." Eira pushed his hands away, took a deep breath and climbed over the gate. Corin followed her, using his shield to protect Eira. Once they were outside Corin noticed there were still men waiting outside of the village. He wondered at that moment if there was a possible way to win this fight.

Corin led Eira into a ditch, unnoticed by the men standing outside. They ran around to the far side of the village and stopped. It was quieter here, and Corin told Eira to sit so he could see if it was safe to leave the ditch. He climbed up the steep slope, which was difficult as the slope was designed to be hard to climb. Laying on the slope, Corin peered over the top. There were iron men all around the village. Corin let out an oath and slid down the hill again.

"We will have to stay here," Corin said quietly. Eira grabbed his hand and pulled him down next to where she was sitting. She curled up next to him and lay her head on his shoulder. He could tell she was crying so he put his arm around her to comfort her. He felt like crying himself. He kissed the top of her head and turned to watch the top of the hill for enemies. His sword was still in the man he had pinned to the wall and he had no spear, but he needed to protect his family. He stared until his eyes were tired, he started to blink as the bright sun started to hurt his eyes.

Corin startled awake, he chastised himself for falling asleep. Eira was also asleep, her head on his lap and she was curled up next to him. He looked down at her, her hair was tangled and her face was covered in dirt. He put his hand on her head and let out a long sigh. He then realized what it was that had woken him. There was no longer a sound of fighting.

Corin looked up and saw smoke billowing out of the village. They were burning it down. The village warriors had lost. Toutatis had failed them. Corin felt tears coming down his cheek, he let himself cry since no one was watching. He moved his hand from Eira's head and put it on her side. He thought briefly about waking Eira and finding a way out but decided it would be best to wait until darkness came.

He felt Eira's side rise and fall as she breathed. She had survived. Likely they were the only two who had, they could move away from here and join another village to fight the iron men. As he sat there a sudden noise made him look upwards. At the top of the slope, he saw the helmet of one of the iron men.

The man uttered something but Corin couldn't understand what he said. Corin realized he was using a different tongue. Corin had heard of men using different words to talk but had never really heard it. He gently shook Eira to wake her, she startled awake and looked up to see the iron man and screamed. This made the iron man laugh. The iron man beckoned Corin and Eira up with his hands.

Corin was trapped and unsure of what to do. He looked around for another way out, Eira had calmed quickly and was looking to him for help. Corin realized he couldn't go back to the village and there was no easy way out of this ditch. Surrender was the only option.

"We will go with him now," Corin explained softly. I will find a way to escape."

# Chapter 7

Corin looked up at the sky, the constant movement of the floor of this boat made him sick. The last several days they had been taken from the village to the shore and put onto this boat. A Gaul named Felix had been put in charge of his group. He could speak the tongues of both groups. Felix explained that they were Romani, from the great city of Roma.

Felix had been to Roma; he was taken from Gaul a few years ago and kept as a slave. He explained to the small group with Corin and Eira that they were selected to go to Roma to be sold there. On hearing that his Eira grabbed hold of Corin, her fingers digging into his arm. Corin had been glad she had because his knees went weak, they had ended up supporting each other.

They were on a boat now, crammed together under the hot sun. They had no shelter and were given very little food and water. Eira had cried the entire first day, and Corin had sat silently wishing he too could cry. He needed to stay strong for her. The floor lurched under him again and he quietly cursed Toutatis for failing to protect them.

Felix had taught them some Romani words, and Corin had found it easy to use them. He suggested to Eira that they review some of the words together. It helped pass the time and keep their minds off the loss of their freedom. Eira gave him a weak smile, appreciative of his effort to help.

"What is Domine?" Corin asked.

"The people in charge," Eira said.

"It means master," a sullen woman sitting close to them muttered. They had been stuck with the same people for this whole journey. They never bothered to learn names; it never crossed their mind. Corin called this woman the negative one, as she never said anything positive. Corin knew things looked bad, but he hated focusing on that.

"Right," Corin said. Eira put her hand on Corin's hand. She knew he was trying to help her get through the loss of her family and appreciated it.

"What is tunica?" Eira asked.

"Clothes," Corin answered. Corin looked down at the simple tunic the Romani had given him. They had forced him to give up his clothes and put on this simple tunic that went just past his knees. He was given no trousers or undergarments and felt very exposed. "Your tunica is beautiful," Corin said with a smile. Eira gave a little half smile, her lips upturning even though her eyes were still sad.

"It is not," she said.

"Aqua?" Corin asked looking out to the horizon.

"Water," Eira said, "all we see is aqua!" Corin laughed softly. The negative woman glared at them. She had often commented that she couldn't understand these two young people.

"You are slaves!" she constantly reminded them, "all you have is gone." Corin and Eira knew this, but they still had each other. Most of the time they quietly mourned their family, friends and home. However, they also felt they needed to try to keep their spirits up. Corin's father had taught him if you keep yourself from falling into despair you are more likely to find a way out of whatever situation you are in.

Eira shifted so she could lay her head on Corin's chest and look out at all the aqua. She sighed and tried not to think of her mother again. When she thought of her, she could picture the sword from the Romani warrior cutting into her.

She held the tears back and turned her head to bury it in Corin's chest. He put a hand on her head and held her tight.

A Romani man stood where he could be seen by all the people huddled on the deck of the boat. He was yelling something in his language, and Felix was brought forward to translate.

"We arrive in Gaul soon," Felix said, "you will get off the boat there. Some of you will be left there while others will be taken to Roma." Eira gasped at this news.

"What if we are separated?" Eira asked Corin.

"You will be," the lady close to them muttered. Corin moved so he could look Eira in the eyes.

"I will find you," Corin said, "you are my betrothed and we belong together." The lady close to them let out a bitter laugh. Eira kissed Corin and thanked him. She knew deep down there was little he could do, but she felt better knowing he would stay with her if he could.

It still felt like a long time before the boat landed in Gaul, but they did finally arrive. The Romani forced them all to stand and get into straight lines, marching them off the boat. Corin and Eira were put into separate lines but could still see each other. They stood in their lines in the hot sun as Romani men walked down the line, stopping at each person and inspecting them.

One man stopped next to Corin and looked at him like he would look at a sheep he was trying to buy. Corin felt the man's rough hands touching him, up and down his arms, squeezing his muscles. Touching his back and legs and then the man grabbed him between his legs. Corin let out a breath and tried to ignore the rough hands.

"You job?" the Romani asked in Corin's own tongue.

"Warrior!" Corin exclaimed. The man turned to a Gaul who was standing with him. He asked for a translation, when the Gaul told him what the word meant he laughed. He said something in Romani and told the Gaul to translate.

"Not anymore," the Gaul said, "do you know sheep or hogs?"

"Sheep," Corin said.

"Anyone else that asks, tell them 'pastor es'," the Gaul told him. He turned to the Romani and told him Corin was a shepherd. The Romani grabbed his arm roughly and dragged him to another line. He lost sight of Eira for a moment but found her again. A Romani man was touching her and talking to her. Corin felt the blood rush to his face, he was ready to go to and defend her but the sight of several Romani men with swords made him rethink that.

He watched and felt a quick sense of relief as the man dragged her to the same line as he was in. They wouldn't be close to each other, but at least they should end up in the same place. This sorting process took a long time and Corin's legs were tired from standing in one spot for so long.

Finally, a slave brought a chain alongside them, along the chain were big pieces that looked like bracelets. The slave put the bracelets around the ankles of each person along the line. The metal was sharp and felt cold against his skin. Every time Corin moved it rubbed against his skin. After everyone was connected with the long chain they were forced to start walking. Corin had no idea where they were going, but they were going together.

They walked for so many days that each day ran into the next. When they started, it was difficult because someone would step wrong and throw the whole chain into chaos as people fell into each other. Finally, they found a rhythm, and everyone walked in unison. It was hot, they had little food and each step hurt as the metal constantly rubbed his ankle. They walked and slept chained together. Corin finally understood why he was not given anything to wear under his tunic. He could not find a place to relieve himself; he just went as they walked. If he had trousers on that would not have been good.

Corin caught the occasional glimpse of Eira as they stopped for the night or when he turned to look behind him. She looked as miserable as he felt. Her skin was red from being exposed to the sun. Her ears sticking out from under her hair were peeling from the damage done.

The worst day, if that were possible to measure, was the day the woman in front of him collapsed onto the cobblestone road they were walking on. The Romani guards had not noticed for a time, and she was just dragged along, the people around her stumbling and trying not to step on her. The people were calling out and finally the progression was stopped. The woman was dead, so the Romani removed her bracelet and pushed her to the side of the road. She was shoved into the ditch and left for the wild animals.

This was a terrible way to treat someone, Corin felt her death deeply even though he didn't know her. Some nights he would have nightmares about Eira or himself being left in a ditch. He knew some others died on the journey, but nobody that was close to him in the line. Even death became nothing to him eventually. Some days he wished death would come for him so he could stop the constant pain. The only thing that kept him going was the idea that he needed to rescue Eira.

The further they walked the more wagons, horses and people they saw on the path. The path was covered in stones, the Romani people called it a 'via,' which meant straight path. They finally came to the city of Roma. There were many great halls, and they stood taller than he could imagine a hall could be. There were people everywhere as well. Many of them wore long strips of cloth instead of a tunic. Other people wore tunics like the one he wore. Corin could not keep his head still as he stared at all the people and halls lining the pathway.

Each building was held up with pillars of stone instead of wood. Corin imagined it would take a lot of work to build such a place. Every person he passed turned their head as if to try to ignore him. They seemed to not want to be a part of whatever he was experiencing. He didn't blame them.

They finally walked through a gate to a large area with columns all around it. There was no roof, but they had small huts here with all kinds of food. People seemed to be trading for food, but Corin couldn't make out what they were trading with. He tried to understand the words being said, and he had learned many more on the walk, but still didn't understand the people here.

They came to a large wooden area with poles that had ropes hanging from them. Corin had a bad feeling about this place. They were taken to a small room and finally the bracelets were removed. Corin quickly found Eira and held her. Her lips were dry and chapped, but felt wonderful when he kissed them. The door opened and two people were roughly grabbed and taken out of the small room. They could hear people calling out words Corin couldn't understand.

"They are selling us," one of the others in the room said. Eira looked up at Corin, her eyes wet with tears.

"I will find you," Corin said firmly. Eira just nodded her head. They stood there in each other's arms as people were dragged out of the room. Finally, Corin felt a rough hand grab his shoulder and he was dragged out the door. To his alarm he felt his tunic being pulled over his head, exposing him. He immediately covered his nakedness with his hands as he was pulled onto the wooden area. The man grabbed his arms and used the ropes attached to the poles to tie his arms above his head. Corin looked out at the crowd, men and women just walking by, ignoring his shame.

Corin heard crying behind him and turned to see Eira being pulled onto the platform, her hands covering herself as well. He didn't want to add to her shame, so he looked at the pole he was tied to. As he stared at pole, he felt rough hands touching his arms and back. There was a man looking at him and talking to the man that had tied him to the pole.

"Quid scis?" the second man asked Corin. He wasn't sure of the second word but knew it was a question, so he guessed its meaning.

"Pastor es," Corin said quietly. All he wanted was for the humiliation to end. The man touched him again and the two men spoke quickly again. He was untied and a tunic was placed over his head again. Corin put it back on with relief. The guard pulled him away and Corin noticed the second man was walking over to Eira.

He watched as the man ran a hand over her back. Eira was weeping loudly at this humiliation, and Corin could barely stand it. When the man's hand got lower Corin lost his temper. He pushed away from the guard and leapt towards Eira and the man. He managed to push the man away from Eira before everything went black.

# Chapter 8

Eira stood tied to the pole, humiliated in front of Corin and all these men. As one man touched her, she saw Corin leap to defend her. The guard hit him on the head with a club, and he collapsed onto the ground. The man who Corin had pushed was laughing, he looked at Eira again. He spoke with the guard and Eira was untied and given her tunic again. As she was pulled away, she saw Corin move, at least he was alive.

Eira was led by that hideous man who had touched her to a wagon close to the place where Corin was laying. There was a woman standing by the wagon wearing a tunic like Eira's but clean. She gave Eira a smile.

"The worst is over," the woman said in Eira's tongue. "I'm Rianwen, but the Romani cannot say that easily. The call me Riana."

"You are from Briton?" Eira asked.

"Yes," Riana responded, the man glared at her so she shushed Eira "get in, we will talk later." Eira sat on a bench in the back of the wagon and Riana pointed to the floor, so she quickly got down. As she sat there, two men carried Corin over and threw him into the wagon. Eira moved to his side and checked him. He had a lump growing on the back of his head; but nothing else seemed wrong. Riana noticed how she cared for him and gave them a sad smile.

The wagon ride through Roma was bumpy and dark as there were no windows to look out. Riana sat on the bench and looked down at the young couple. At last, she could talk.

"What's your name girl?" Riana asked.

"I'm Eira," Eira replied, "what is going on?"

"We are returning to the domus of your new master," Riana said, "Marcus Fabius Sabinus, he's a fair master, if you work hard, you will be rewarded. Your young friend will be going to the fields, and you will work in the villa." Eira let out a whimper.

"You are lucky," Riana said, "I was brought here with my mother, I've not seen her again. She was sold to someone else."

"Will I be able to see Corin?" Eira asked hopefully, "we are promised."

"The domus is in town, and the villa is a long walk from there," Riana said. "You might not be able to see each other, but you have hope." Eira looked down at Corin's face. Hope. At this point she had lost all hope. Corin told her he would rescue her, but how if they were far apart? Eira let herself cry quietly.

When the wagon stopped, Riana told Eira to say farewell to Corin. He was still not responding so Eira kissed his lips and got out of the wagon. It left almost as soon as she was out. Eira watched and tried to hope she would see Corin again.

Riana led her into the villa where the man she now knew was Marcus Fabius Sabinus stood. He said something in Romani, and Eira understood enough to answer in the same tongue.

"I am Eira," she said. The man laughed, it wasn't a mean laugh like she was expecting, but warm and kind.

"You speak Latīna?" Marcus Fabius asked.

"A little," Eira answered. "I was taught on the…" Eira didn't know the word for boat, so she switched to her own tongue. Riana and translated the word for her. Eira listened and tried to put the new word in her memory.

"You learn quickly," Marcy's Fabius said, "come and meet my wife." Eira didn't understand the whole of what was said and Riana translated. They walked through a large doorway into the domus. Eira noticed that the door was opened by another slave who had a small room by the door.

"That is Brisca," Riana said, "they call him Prisca. He's the ostiarius, he guards the door." As they walked in Eira could not believe what she was looking at. The room was tall with a flat roof made of the same material as the walls. It was hard and colorful material. The floors were made of stone, not dirt, and the stones were set out in a pattern.

They walked into a beautiful room with plants surrounding a pool that was under an opening to the sky. There was a small bed there, and a lady was half laying on the bed. She was dressed in a long strip of cloth with a light tunic underneath. She wore leather shoes that had an intricate design of leather straps going up her leg. Eira had noticed that Marcus Fabius wore similar shoes. Her hair was sitting on her head in a way that Eira couldn't imagine possible. She had a plait, but it seemed to be wrapped around her hair and lifting some of it. Her lips were as red as Eira's skin was. She was beautiful.

"This is Domina Flavius Sabina," Riana said. "You will work for her." Eira was happy to know that she would work for a woman. She felt that Marcus Flavius was kind, but she could still feel his rough hands on her backside. She wasn't sure how to greet her new mistress, so she stepped forward and lowered her eyes.

Marcus and Flavia exchanged words so fast that Eira couldn't follow what was being said. Riana explained that the last girl he had brought Flavia had a crooked back. Marcus explained that he had inspected this one and she was fine. Realization struck Eira that this was why he had touched her back. He was making sure he wouldn't make the same mistake. While she still hated what happened it felt a little better to have some understanding.

After a while, Flavia beckoned Eira forward. She touched Eira's back and nodded. She must have been satisfied, and Marcus left quickly and Eira was left with just the women.

"Come," Flavia said, "we must clean you." Again, the word 'clean' was not one she was familiar with. Raina translated and Eira followed with some curiosity. They walked further into the domus. They passed several rooms that were all beautiful and came to a small passageway. Flavia stood by the entrance to the passageway and indicated that Eira should enter. Riana guided her in.

"This is the slave corridor," Riana explained, "the Domina will not come in here unless she must." It was narrow and not as beautiful, but finally they came to a room with several mats on the floor. In one corner was a big clay basin. Riana directed her to the basin.

"I'm sorry," Raina explained, "but I must wash you to the Romani custom. You will learn to do it yourself soon. The Romani are very clean people. They want slaves to be the same."

Riana helped Eira remove her tunic and helped her wash herself using water from the basin. She had a curved metal tool that she used to scrape dirt from her skin, it hurt the areas where the sun had damaged her skin. Afterwards, Riana covered her skin with oils that smelled wonderful. The oils soothed her burnt skin. Eira started to enjoy the feeling, forgetting the humiliation of being washed.

"Your hair," Riana said, "I'm afraid we must cut it."

"Cut it?" Eira said, "but I've never cut it!"

"Yes," Riana said, "it will grow back, but we must cut it very short to check for insects."

"Insects?" Eira cried, "I have none!"

"I must be sure," Raina tutted, "please." Eira sat on the ground and allowed Raina to cut her hair very short. Afterwards Riana put a white powder on her head to kill the lice she had. She had not believed they were there, when Raina told her about them but the powder stung so maybe they were there. After this Eira was given a new tunic. It was still plain and white, but it was softer than her old one. She was also given underclothes, which was the small blessing in this whole situation.

Eira was led back out to Domina Flavia, who nodded with approval. Flavia led Eira back to the main entrance and told her to wait by the pool. She stood there with Riana wondering what humiliation would come next. She heard it before she saw it; the sound of a child rushing down the hall. A young girl rushed into the room and stopped when she saw Eira.

"Mama!" the girl said as Flavia entered, "she has ears like a jug!" Eira felt the blood rush to her face. Flavia pushed the girl closer. She was dressed similarly to her mother, but her hair was done in two braids down her back. She had a small nose and freckles across the bridge. Her lips were small, but Eira knew her mouth was big.

"This is your new assistant," Flavia explained, "by the gods I don't know your name! Tell me girl!"

"Eira," shyly Eira looked at the girl.

"What a barbaric name! We will never be able to say that" Flavia said, "you will be Ennia." Riana translated some of the words so Eira could understand she needed to answer to 'Ennia' now.

"Ennia, this is Flavia Druscilla," Flavia announced, pointing at the girl. "You will watch over her. Raina will teach you." With that Flavia turned and left the room, leaning Eira and Raina with Druscilla.

The rest of the day was a blur as Raina showed Eira around the villa and explained her new role. She was to help the girl dress in the morning, escort her around and keep her from bothering the adults, fetch her food and get her to bed at night. After she slept, Eira had to clean any mess she made in the day and clean her clothes and mend any damaged clothing. After all that was done she would sleep on the floor by Druscilla's bed.

The main room Eira was responsible for was the cubiculum of Druscilla. It was a large room, bigger than the roundhouse that Eira had lived in her whole life. The floor had those colorful stones; they had an intricate pattern on them. Eira was told the floor must be always kept clean. Druscilla's bed was a tall platform that was soft on top. She had several wool blankets for warmth. Eira would have a mat on the floor with a single wool blanket.

There was a cabinet with doors on it that stood in the corner of the cubiculum. Inside were clothes and toys for the little girl. This was to be kept organized the way it was now. The clothing that was soiled cold be washed in the culina, or kitchen where there was warm water. Cleanliness was the most important.

Raina took Eira and Druscilla to another room, to teach Eira about Romani cleanliness. There were four sections in this room, they walked into the first and a slave was waiting for them. Raina removed Druscilla's clothing and handed them to the slave, who folded them neatly and put them on a shelf. He handed them a folded cloth that Raina put around the girl, showing Eira how to do it properly.

The second room had shelves with that little tool for scraping the skin and vials of different oils. Raina showed Eira how to scrape the child's skin carefully to remove dirt. Eira was amazed at how the child stood still and allowed Raina to scrape her skin. Afterwards, Eira was shown which oils were needed to keep her skin healthy.

The next room was impossibly hot, with steam coming out of the floor. There was a large pool in the middle of the room. Druscilla took off her cloth and went into the pool on her own.

"You must take care that she does not splash or play in here," Raina explained. Eira wasn't quite sure why this was a rule but was determined to learn all the rules of this strange place quickly. Druscilla stepped out of the pool and allowed Raina to drape her again. Eira noticed that there was another slave in this room and wondered how he managed to stay in this heat all day. The last room had another larger pool of water and Druscilla again disrobed and went into the pool on her own. After she moved around in this water for a little while, she got out again. Eira noticed that the water in this pool was very cold. They went back through a corridor to the first room where they got the girl dressed again.

Eira understood her responsibility but was a little overwhelmed by the strange customs. The girl was very young and would be easy to care for, Eira had cared for cousins before and enjoyed it. That had been at home, with customs and rules she understood. She wasn't sure she would ever be able to learn all this or find her way around the villa. Riana promised her that she would manage, everyone did eventually.

That first night in Druscilla's room was lonely. Eira thought back to the time on the boat. She had been sad and sacred, but she had Corin with her. Now she was alone on a small mat on the floor by the bed of a child. The child who was by all accounts her master. Eira fell asleep in a pool of her own tears.

# Chapter 9

Corin woke with a sharp pain in the back of his head. Someone had hit him so hard he had fallen unconscious. Corin slowly opened his eyes and looked out. There was hay all around him, was he home? Had he dreamed the whole thing? Maybe he had fallen in the storeroom and hit his head. He sat up, he was in a pile of hay, but he wasn't at home. The room he was in was larger than any storeroom he had ever seen. Piles of hay were stacked around him, more than he could imagine any one family needing.

Corin lay back and tried to remember what had happened. Then it came to him, Eira's exposed body and that man touching her. He had pushed the man and been clubbed for his actions. Corin stood up and saw the same man standing just outside the entryway. He started to walk towards him when the pain in his ankle grew sharp again. He looked down and saw that he was chained up. Again.

The man heard him and stared walking towards Corin. He might have his chance to beat this man. As the man got closer, Corin launched himself forward, but the chain pulled him back.

"You said you were a shepherd," the man said with a laugh. "You seem to be a wolf." Corin didn't understand the last word but took its meaning from context.

"Where is Eira?" Corin managed in the Romani tongue. Laughing again the man beckoned over a man that Corin realized was Felix, the Gaul slave. Felix recognized Corin and said something to the evil man in his tongue. Corin heard his own name and the word he knew to mean 'woman.' The

Romani man laughed again and told Felix something that Corin didn't understand.

"Your girl is safe," Felix said, "he did not know she was married. She is very young."

"We are promised," Corin said quietly. Felix explained everything to the man who nodded solemnly, the laugh gone. He said something more and Felix nodded and turned to explain.

"You, of course, are too young to marry," Felix said, "but he understands what it is to be promised. He met his wife when she was only ten," Felix paused, he had to think of an equivalent to a word he had gotten used to using, "ten summers. Very young."

"Eira has had thirteen summers," Corin said proudly. "I believe." Felix translated and the man said something that made Felix laugh. Corin tried hard to understand, but only caught the word for 'barbarian,' something he was called many times since capture.

"He says he hopes barbarians can wait for a respectable age to marry," Felix explained. "I told him you had at least two more years to wait."

"We are promised," Corin said again, "we should be married." Felix nodded but did not translate.

"Domine Marcus Fabius Sabine owns you both," Felix explained, "your girl is in the domus caring for his daughter. If he doesn't sell one of you before you become of age, you can petition to marry."

"Good," Corin said.

"Not good," Felix said, "I spoke with the head slave here. He's a Judean, he knows everything that goes on. Apparently, your love is to care for his daughter. He said that their daughter has gone through five girls already. She's only six summers but doesn't like any girl and her father does what she likes. The last one supposedly had a crooked back and gave her bad dreams. If she lasts for a season I would be impressed." Corin let his face fall, and Felix told him to smile or the Domine might guess he was sharing personal gossip.

Corin dug deep inside of himself not to cry out in anguish and tried to smile. He would have to do what he could to get to Eira before then and escape. He looked at the chain and realized he would need to seem trustworthy first.

"What does my Domine want?" Corin managed in the Romani tongue. Felix smiled and turned to his master.

"You said you are a shepherd," the Domine said, "I need someone to care for my sheep." Felix translated, but Corin had already understood some of it.

"Yes, Domine," Corin said. The thought of being able to watch sheep appealed to him. It was something he was used to and he knew how to keep them healthy and alive.

"There are wolves in this area," the Domine said sternly, when Felix translated Corin shook his head to show he wasn't worried.

"I have killed wolves before," Corin said. He then smiled and added in his own tongue, "it would be easier if I had my spear." Felix translated and the Domine let out a loud laugh.

"I would be afraid you would come and kill me in my sleep," the Domine said. Corin just smiled at him and said nothing. The Domine looked down his long nose at Corin and said "I will call you Lupinus." He then told Felix to bring his head slave over to free him from his chains and set him to work. He added to wait for him to get to safety and laughed at his own joke. The Domine left quickly and Felix told Corin to wait. He didn't have much choice, so he sat and waited a short while. Felix returned with a shorter man with dark hair and dark skin.

"This is Josephus," Felix said, "he will remove the chain." Josephus carefully took the chain off Corin's ankle. Corin sat down and rubbed the spot where the chain had been. Josephus then led Corin to a field where there were about a hundred sheep.

"These are the Domine's sheep," Josephus said, "you are to take care of them. You have done this before?"

"Since I was small," Corin said. Josephus looked at Corin who stood a whole head taller than him and smiled.

"You were small?" Josephus asked, "you are like the story of Golyat, but you are a shepherd like Daud." He laughed as his little joke as he walked. Corin felt like he understood the words but still didn't understand what he meant.

"I am still learning the tongue," Corin said, "what did you mean?"

"It is a story from my people," Josephus said, "the shepherd boy that beat a big man, like you, in battle." Corin needed Felix to translate but nodded once he heard it. People were the same everywhere, they told the stories of their heroes. He appreciated that they also had shepherds who became warriors.

Corin walked among the sheep, touching their wool and he felt an immediate sense of calm. He would get to know these sheep the same way he knew his fathers sheep back home. They looked healthy and well fed, Corin knew he would have an easy job caring for them.

Josephus took Corin on a walk of the land where he could take the sheep to graze. The ground had some hills and valleys, but the valleys were not very deep. There were no forests, but there were trees scattered in the hills. Corin took note of the landmarks and water available. Josephus explained that in this area sometimes the water dried up. Josephus showed him where the Romani had built their own river. It was a tall structure but had places where the water could be collected to give to the sheep. Corin had to admit it was nice to have a guaranteed source of water.

The sun was getting low as Corin returned to the storeroom with the hay. He would be sleeping here with the sheep. A slave brought him a plate with some bread and a potage that was very runny and had some strange grain in it. Corin ate hungrily and then settled down. As he lay there listening to the sounds of the sheep moving around, Corin wondered how Eira was doing.

The last time he had seen her she was tied to a pole, humiliated and crying. Corin was happy with where he had ended up and hoped Eira had the same fortune.

# Part II

## The Journey Home
## (5 years later)

# Chapter 10

"Ennia!" Eira rushed down the corridor to find the Domina standing in Druscilla's cubicula with the girl standing in front of her. Eira noticed that the girl had apparently removed the tunic Eira had put her in and put on one that had not been washed yet. It still had food stains from the day before. "Where were you?" Domina asked.

"I had to relieve myself," Eira gasped, a little out of breath. The slaves had a toilet at the back of the domus by the culina. She was glad of that because the Romani had no concept of modesty. One time, as she was washing Druscilla in the bath the Domine walked in and removed his tunic and got into the water. Eira realized she was staring at him, but she was disgusted by this action. She learned to always avert her eyes as he came in.

"Why is she wearing this?" Domina asked.

"I'm very sorry," Eira said, looking at the floor. She was hoping that she wouldn't get hit for this mistake. Her only mistake was leaving Druscilla alone. Fortunately, the Domina had other matters to deal with and just told Eira to correct her mistake.

After the Domina left Eira picked up the tunic she had selected for Druscilla. It was beautiful and had an ornate neckline and sleeves. She picked it up and rushed to help Druscilla get changed.

"Why did you take this off?" Eira asked.

"It's ugly," the girl said staring at the offending garment. Eira looked at the colorful ribbon on the neck and shook her head. This girl was given the finest clothing and always wanted simple clothes.

"Your mother wants you to wear this," Eira said, "today's an important day." Druscilla looked at Eira, her eyes full of trepidation. This was the day Druscilla was going to meet the boy her father had selected for her to marry when she came of age.

"Do you remember the day you met your betrothed?" Druscilla asked. Eira smiled as she helped the girl remove her stained tunic and put on the ornate one.

"I remember the day we were promised," Eira said thoughtfully, "not the day we met. I've known him as far back as I can remember." Druscilla knit her brow as she thought about that. Today she was meeting the boy she was supposed to marry, she didn't know him. He was the second son of a senator, so his family was very important in Roma. Her father had made this arrangement to win some influence in the senate.

"What if he's ugly," Druscilla asked.

"He's a boy," Eira said, "they're all ugly." Druscilla laughed, Eira did not believe this, but Druscilla said it all the time. The first time she used the word, Eira had not understood so Druscilla helped her understand by making an ugly face. This had made Eira laugh, she might be this girl's slave, but they had become close over the years.

"What about Lupinus?" Druscilla said with a grin. Eira had pointed Corin out when they had visited the villa. Her heart leapt when she saw him out with the sheep. They were never allowed close enough to talk as the Domina didn't want a shepherd close to her daughter. Eira made it into a game where the girls could see how close they could get to Corin without anyone noticing.

"He is very handsome," Eira said, her face starting to blush. "Let's do your hair quickly and finish getting dressed." Druscilla sat down and let Eira brush and plait her hair. Eira wrapped the plait around the girl's head the way the Domina insisted. She then helped her with her cloak, or palla as they called it. As they finished the Domina walked into the room.

"Very well-done Druscilla," Domina said, "you will please your father and your betrothed." Eira took this as high praise for her work. As mother and daughter left to go to the atrium, Eira followed a step behind them.

As they entered the atrium, the Domine was standing with a strange man in a white toga. This must be the senator, next to him was a boy who looked very embarrassed to be here. He had a long face and long nose but wasn't unattractive. Eira hoped Druscilla would see him that way. Druscilla looked back at Eira and gave her a small smile. She liked how he looked, Eira thanked the gods.

The exchange between the adults was brief, all agreements were completed a long time ago. The senator introduced his son Titus Septimius Marcellus and Marcus Fabius introduced his daughter Druscilla Favia. It was all very formal. The betrothed were allowed to greet each other and then Eira was told to take Druscilla back to her room.

On the way back Druscilla laughed and turned to Eira. "Don't you think, he's handsome?" Druscilla asked.

"Yes," Eira said, "he is very handsome." Druscilla did a little dance as she walked ahead of Eira. She seemed to be very happy with the results of the day. Eira had found it all very different to the day she had been promised, but the results seemed to be the same. Druscilla was looking forward to getting married.

When they got back to her cubicula, Druscilla asked Eira to help her change into clothes she liked. Since the formal event was as over Eira obliged her. The rest of the day Druscilla was supposed to have lessons, so comfortable clothes were in order.

Eira escorted Druscilla over to her lessons with her private teacher. This was one of Eira's favorite parts of the day. She had been taking Druscilla to lessons since they started several years ago. Eira had learned to read and write along with her young ward. She had also learned Latīna so she could speak like a Romani.

When they arrived at the lesson, Druscilla's tutor congratulated her. It was a special moment for a girl to know her future was secure. Druscilla beamed in all the attention. As they were working, they could hear the celebration coming from the atrium. The adults were celebrating the betrothal. It seemed odd to Eira that Druscilla wasn't involved, but she had learned long ago that the way the Romani did things was very different from the Briton way.

After the lesson, Druscilla was to eat and then bathe. Eira walked to the kitchen to get the food. Josephus, the head slave from the villa, was sitting in the kitchen. Eira greeted him formally and started to put together the food for Druscilla.

"Your man sends greetings," Josephus said to Eira. Eira's heart leapt, all their communication had gone through this man since they had joined this household. He was an odd little man who seemed to enjoy his role.

"Thank you," Eira said, "return my greetings. Let him know I am doing well." Josephus smiled and walked over to Eira. He put a hand on her shoulder, it felt strangely calming.

"I am praying to my God for you," Josephus said quietly, "may He bring you two together." Eira smiled at her friend. He had talked to her about his God before, he said that he served a single God. Eira said wondered how one God could manage caring for everything. "The Domine has invited the slaves from the villa to have our own celebration of the day. Corin will be here after the sun sets." Eira's heart leapt. Maybe she would be able to see him after Druscilla went to sleep for the night. She had clothes to wash so she had a reason to return to the kitchen.

"Thank you," Eira said.

"May the Mashiach bless your marriage," Josephus said as he walked away. This was another odd thing about Josephus' God; Josephus had met him. He was called the Mashiach and had walked among men. Josephus talked about him often, claiming to have met him as a boy.

Eira carried the food back to Druscilla's room. She hoped the God Mashiach would bring her and Corin together. Her gods had failed her; she should be married and living with Corin by now. When it was just her and Druscilla her job was pleasant, but any time she interacted with the parents she was afraid of what they would do to her. They didn't beat her often because she was careful, but they had beat her when she was just learning her job.

Druscilla enjoyed eating and ate every meal with enthusiasm. Eira was allowed a few minutes to eat before taking Druscilla to the baths. She ate some lentil stew and bread quickly and thought back to her conversation with Jospehus. Eira wondered about the gods, did they really care about what happened to her? She couldn't imagine that she was important, she was a lowly slave after all. She decided not to put any hope in the prayers to a god she didn't even know.

As she walked behind Druscilla towards the bath she heard the celebration in the atrium. They were still eating and drinking and would likely go on long after she was done her chores and in bed. Druscilla suddenly stopped in her tracks and Eira nearly walked into her.

There was a man dressed in a dark tunic and holding a sword. He smiled at the two ladies and stepped towards them. As he reached out to grab Druscilla, Eira slapped his hand away. He hit her hard and she fell back, landing roughly on the floor. Eira watched in horror as he put his hand on Druscilla's mouth to stifle her screams as he picked her up.

Eira thought about fighting the man when she realized someone else was with him. She couldn't defeat two men. Thinking fast she pretended to faint in fear. One of the men kicked her in the side and she stifled her cry. As soon as she heard them run off, she jumped up and ran into the atrium.

"Someone took Druscilla!" Eira yelled as she entered the atrium. There was so much noise, nobody took notice of her at first. Fortunately, she normally avoided the atrium during celebrations, so her presence attracted her attention of the Domina immediately. The Domina sensed something was wrong and walked over to Eira.

"What did you say?" Domina asked,

"Men came in and took Druscilla!" Eira yelled, trying hard to control her emotions but failing. The Domina's hand went to her mouth and then she screamed for her husband. He left the group he was talking to and rushed over. As soon as she explained what happened, the Domine grabbed some men from nearby and rushed out to find Druscilla.

The Domina fell into Eira's arms in tears as more men rushed out to join the excitement. Another woman came to comfort the Domina and Eira rushed out to help however she could. There were men moving up and down the halls trying to find the kidnappers. Eira decided to let the slaves in the kitchen know what was going on, hoping they could help.

As she rushed down the slave corridor she heard muffled crying from the slaves' quarters. It should be empty with the celebration going on. She tried to decide which was better, to get help or to deal with it herself. She suddenly remembered something Corin had talked about when they were at home. He had mentioned that sometimes knowing you are there puts real fear into an enemy. He had even taught her the battle cry he intended to use to put fear into the enemy.

Eira decided to try a battle cry, it might make the men fearful, and it would let anyone around know something was happening. She made her voice as low as possible and let out a guttural groan, she hadn't done it since she was much younger, when playing with Corin, but it came out loud and clear. As she did this, she found a stool in the hall and picked it up to use as a shield. She had watched the men train with shields as a child, maybe she could at least keep herself alive.

Suddenly a shadow appeared in the entrance to the slaves' quarters. It had to be one of the men, Eira held up her shield and ran at him, using the shield to slam him into the wall. The man grunted and let out a string of oaths. Eira pushed with all her might, but he was stronger and started to push back. As she lost her footing, she saw the other man who was holding Druscilla push by into the corridor. Eira screamed.

She suddenly saw the shadow of a giant man; he had been hiding against the wall. He had a club in his hand and used it to knock out the man holding Druscilla. He then stood between the girl and the man fighting Eira. He gently pushed Eira aside and in that moment, she recognized Corin. She briefly wondered what he was doing here but was glad he was.

Corin picked the other man up with one hand and threw him across the room. The man's sword had fallen when Eira rammed into him and Corin grabbed it and used it to end the fight quickly. The room was suddenly filled with light as Romani men led by the Domine entered the room carrying torches. Eira rushed to Druscilla who was shaken but unhurt.

"Domine," Eira called out, "May I take her to her mother?" The Domine was quickly taking in everything. The dead man's blood was pooling on the floor, and the shepherd boy was standing over the dead body. He nodded quietly and Eira rushed the girl away from everything to her mother's waiting arms.

The Domina wept when she had her daughter safe again. Eira was full of questions but just stood back waiting for further instructions. After a while the Domina told Eira to take her daughter back to her cubiculum. Eira was happy to do so, Druscilla grabbed her hand and wouldn't let go, even though that went against the rules. The Domina saw the action but allowed it.

# Chapter 11

Corin sat at the base of an olive tree and looked out over the sheep in the field. He kept rethinking the night before. He had been invited to join the slaves to celebrate the betrothal of the Domine's daughter. He had hoped to see Eira there but knew she would be with the little Domina the whole time. He had been sitting with Josephus in the kitchen when he heard Eira's battle cry. He had heard it before as a boy and his heart leapt to his throat when he heard it.

Corin had rushed to the corridor to see Eira attacking a man with a stool. He had a club that he used to protect the sheep from wolves and as he was about to help Eira when he saw the other man carrying a girl. Corin quickly decided this man was the biggest threat, so he knocked the man out. Protecting Eira was a simple decision. In his rage he quickly killed the man who had been attacking her. Afterwards, the Domine thanked him and then told him to return to his duty.

Corin had wanted to wait to make sure Eira was not hurt but had to do as told. Now he sat with his sheep, hoping to see Josephus to get some news from the domus. He couldn't be certain he would hear any news; he wasn't important enough. He stood up and walked through the herd of sheep, silently counting and checking to make sure they were all healthy. As he finished his walk, he noticed Jospehus out by the ovile, the building he had originally called the storeroom.

Corin made his way over there, herding the sheep as he went. It took time to get them back, but there were wolves out and he didn't want to risk losing any sheep to the predators. As the sheep walked into their home, Corin noticed that Josephus wasn't alone, the Domine was with him. The two men walked over to Corin.

"I named you well, Lupinus," the Domine said. "It was good you were in the villa last night."

"Thank you," Corin said, "how is your daughter?"

"She was not hurt," the Domine responded. "Flavia Sabinus has taken her for a picnic. She always enjoys outings." Corin nodded, he wasn't aware of anything that went on in the domus, the concept of a picnic was foreign to him. He really wanted to ask about Eira but felt he couldn't.

"Ennia is also unhurt," Josephus added to Corin's relief. "She has asked about you, but we can talk later." Josephus looked at their Domine and Corin understood. He could wait a few minutes. Let the Domine thank him and then have a real conversation.

"The Domina says I am to offer you a reward," the Domine said. Corin felt that he didn't really understand. He understood Latīna well now; but some words were still new to him. He looked from the Domine to Josephus blankly.

"He wants to know if there is anything you want," Jospehus explained. Corin wasn't sure what exactly to say, so he just said what was always in his heart.

"I want to marry Eira," he paused and remembered they had given her a new name, "Ennia, I want to marry Ennia." The Domine laughed, but it wasn't a cruel laugh.

"I think we can make that possible," the Domine said. "But you are here and she is in the villa. How will you ever see each other?"

"One day together will be wonderful," Corin said, his heart beating hard in his chest. The Domine laughed again.

"It has been years," the Domine said, "will she still want to marry you?"

"I can assure you," Josephus said, "she has been promised to him and wishes to keep that promise." Corin looked at his Judean friend, he had passed so many messages over the years and knew they loved each other. Corin looked at the Domine, feeling like he was begging for his very life.

"One day is enough with my wife," the Domine said with a bawdy laugh. "However, I think you will want more. As your reward I am moving you to the domus, you will work there and I will allow the marriage." Corin looked at the sheep. He was a shepherd, what could he do in the domus. Josephus saw the look, he smiled at Corin as if to say all would be explained.

The Domine walked off, finished with this conversation. Josephus followed but turned to Corin and held up a finger to indicate that he would be back. Corin sat on some hay and wondered what was going on. He thought he understood that somehow, he would be able to move to the villa and marry Eira.

By the time Josephus had returned, Corin had convinced himself that he had misunderstood the whole conversation. Josephus sat next to him, grinning from ear to ear.

"Do you know the job of an ostiarius?" Corin shook his head. Since arriving he had been to the domus very few times. "They keep watch over the entry to the villa," Josephus explained. "Last night the ostiarius was killed by the men who tried to take Druscilla. He was getting older and should have been moved from that role anyway."

"So that will be my new job?" Corin asked quietly.

"Yes," Josephus said, "starting today. Felix will watch the sheep until a new slave is bought. We need someone to guard the entrance, and who better than Lupinus, the wolf man?" Corin stood up and looked towards the city. He would be in the same house as Eira soon.

As Corin had no belongings, they left immediately for the villa. The walk was unreal as Corin looked around at all the people in the city. Nobody paid them any attention, just two slaves walking through town. As the domus came closer Corin was sure he was dreaming.

The room next to the entryway was small, but it was better than the ovile. A young slave was scrubbing the tiles on the floor, the dark red stain of blood still visible despite her efforts. Josephus explained his role; Corin was to live in this room and stop anyone that tried to enter. He would soon know who was welcome and who to turn away. Josephus would stay close by to help the first few days.

"Who is this?" the Domina asked from the entry to the small room. She had just returned from her picnic with Druscilla to find a strange new ostiarius. Corin looked out and his heart leapt to see Eira a step behind them. She was not looking at them and hadn't seen him yet.

"This is Lupinus," Jospehus said brightly, Eira's head turned at the name, she nearly cried out when she saw Corin there. "He is the one who rescued Domina Druscilla. Domine Marcus Fabius has rewarded him with position as ostiarius." Druscilla recognized him and cried out.

"Oh! Ennia!" Druscilla said, "he's here!" The Domina turned to her daughter.

"You know this man?" the Domina asked.

"She is Ennia's betrothed!" Druscilla exclaimed. The Domina looked and Eira, whose red face betrayed the truth.

"How is this possible?" the Domina asked, "have you been sneaking out?"

"No Domina!" Eira said, "we have been betrothed since childhood. We were captured when our village was destroyed."

"Captured together?" the Domina said, "how unfortunate for you. Still, I suppose you will want to be married. I will speak to my husband." Corin was about to say something and Josephus put and hand on his forearm to stop him.

"You are so kind," Josephus said, "thank you Domina." The Domina smiled and bowed her head slightly. Josephus gave Corin's arm a pat, Corin realized what his friend was doing, instead of telling the Domina that the wedding was arranged, he had allowed her to think it was her idea. She was so pleased with herself for coming up with the idea. Corin could see why people trusted Josephus, he understood people.

"Come," the Domina said, "we must go and prepare for our bath. I always feel so dusty after a trip out." Corin watched as the three ladies walked into the villa. Eira put a hand out and he grabbed it for a second as she passed by.

"That is good," Josephus said, "she will be helpful in preparing your wedding."

"Why did you let her think it was her idea?" Corin asked.

"It was," Josephus said with a grin, "she just wasn't the first person to have it." Josephus excused himself to go take care of a few things. He told Corin that nobody was expected today but to call him if anyone came and he would let him know what to do.

Corin sat on the bench built into the entryway for the ostiarius. He looked out into the street; he would soon be able to marry Eira. He had no way of knowing how that would work, he was to sleep here, and she was to sleep in the girl's cubiculum. He didn't care right now, right now he allowed himself to be happy. He sat watching the people pass by. While he preferred watching sheep, this would be interesting.

# Chapter 12

Eira looked in her reflection in the water of the wash basin. She had changed a lot since arriving, her ears no longer looked like the handles of a jug, and she had grown into her teeth. She put her hand into the water, breaking up the image. She splashed some water onto her face, scrubbing it clean. She then washed the rest of her body and used some oil to make her skin look beautiful.

Today was the day! She was finally going to be married to Corin. The Domina had insisted that it happen soon and had even given them half a day to be together. Druscilla was already dressed and had been taken her to lessons before Eira could get ready herself. Someone else would stay with Druscilla for the second half of the day.

Eira walked down the corridor to the slave quarters where Corin was waiting. The blend of excitement and nerves filled Eira. What if they didn't get along after all these years. She knew she had changed, had he? Josephus confided with her that Corin had been the one to ask the Domine for permission. He wanted this! She wanted it! It had to work out somehow.

Felix had agreed to witness the marriage since he knew their tongue and their customs. They stood hand in hand while Felix wrapped a cord around their wrists. He gave a blessing in their own tongue, which was odd to hear after all these years. Then Corin bent down and kissed her.

The kiss lasted longer than any kiss they had experienced. It was warm and full of love. Eira's neck was starting to hurt from bending his head so far back and she was sure Corin's back must be hurting but she didn't care. When they stopped Felix was smiling, he left the room and closed the door behind them. They were alone.

The slaves all had strict instructions from Josephus to stay away from the slave quarters for the afternoon. They were to have privacy, and they took advantage of the fact they were alone. The time apart melted as Eira threw herself into Corin's arms. Corin looked deep into her eyes, she felt as if he could see her very soul. Slowly he kissed her again as they merged and became one. As the sun started to go down Josephus knocked on the door.

Eira had her head on Corin's chest when the knock came. She sighed, she would love to stay laying with him a little longer, but she had work to do. Druscilla still liked to have her in the room as she fell asleep and Corin would be a better man at the door than Josephus as darkness came. Eira traced the muscles on Corin's arm and Corin answered their supervisor.

"We will be out in a minute," Corin called out as he stood. They dressed quickly and went out to the corridor where Josephus was waiting. He looked at them as a parent would look at a child.

"I'm sorry I couldn't be there for your wedding," Josephus said, "but I wanted to add a blessing from my people." Josephus raised a hand and started to sing in his own tongue; "Baruch ata Adonai, Eloheinu melech ha'olam, asher bara sason v'simcha chatan v'chala. Gila, rina, ditzah v'chedva, ahava v'achava v'shalom v'rei'ut. M'heira Adonai Eloheinu yishama b'arei yehuda u'vchutzot yerushalayim, kol sason v'kol simcha kol chatan v'kol kala, kol mitzhalot chatanim meichupatam u'n'arim mimishtei n'ginatam. Baruch ata Adonai m'sameiach chatan im ha'kala."

Hearing it made Eira's heart feel warm. She could feel a blessing from the gods on her marriage. She reached out and took Corin's hand with her right hand and Jospehus' hand with her left.

"That was truly beautiful," Eira said, "what does it mean?"

"It is a blessing," Josephus said, "that the God of my fathers would give you love and joy, peace and friendship." Josephus leaned in conspiratorially and said, "and many children." Corin chuckled and Eira looked at the two men. She hadn't thought about children. What would happen to a child born to her in slavery? She wanted to ask but was afraid of the answer.

She walked slowly back to Druscilla's room. She had been given the responsibility of caring for somebody else's child, but who would care for her child? She couldn't do this job with a child, could she? Eira got to the entrance to Druscilla's cubiculum and took a deep breath. Druscilla would expect her to be happy, if she were crying, she would likely tell the Domina the marriage was not good. She tried to forget about the prospect of having a child and let her thoughts go back to her time with Corin. The smile came naturally.

The slave who had taken Eira's place was relieved to see her return. She rushed out of the room as soon as she could. The little Domina was playing with her dolls, she liked to make up stories with them. Eira would join in and use silly voices for some of the dolls. Druscilla was getting a little old for such games, but they both loved playing. When Druscilla saw Eira she dropped the dolls and rushed to her.

"How was it?" Druscilla asked.

"It was wonderful," Eira said, directing Druscilla to sit so she could take her hair down. As Eira brushed her hair, Druscilla peppered her with questions about the ceremony and their first kiss. She was still too young to understand everything about what a man and wife did together, so some of the questions amused Eira.

By this time Druscilla was ready for bed, she lay on her bed and stared at the ceiling. Eira hoped she was out of questions when suddenly she sat back up and looked at Eira. Her face was twisted with concern.

"Will your baby replace me?" Druscilla asked. Eira realized the child didn't fully understand the situation. In her mind Eira was her caregiver, her constant companion. She didn't realize that Eira had no choice.

"Don't worry," Eira told Druscilla, petting her hair, "I will care for you as long as you need." Druscilla lay back down and sighed. Eira sat with her, rubbing her back, until she could feel the deep, even breaths of sleep. Eira quietly collected Druscilla's dolls and put them away. She took the dirty clothes and placed them in a basket to take to the kitchen for washing.

As Eira walked to the kitchen with the basket of clothes she thought about her future children. She had been so happy earlier when she and Corin were together, but what if they had already created a child? Eira carefully washed the small tunic and underclothes, hanging them by the fire in the kitchen to dry. She kept putting her hand on her stomach, 'please wait' she pleaded quietly.

Eira couldn't imagine being free from slavery but knew it did happen. They had heard gossip from other households of slaves being granted freedom for some good deed. Eira walked back down the corridor where just a few weeks earlier she had fought the man that had taken Druscilla. She had risked her life for this family. If that didn't give her freedom, nothing would.

Eira checked to ensure that Druscilla was asleep and then went the back way to the entrance. Corin's face lit up when he saw her, he stood from his bench and kissed her. She felt a little better now that she was in his arms again.

"I think I can come here to see you every night once Druscilla is asleep and my work is done," Eira said.

"That is good," Corin said. He pointed to a chain coiled in the corner. "The ostiarius are often chained here so they don't leave. It appears the Domine trusts me. I don't want him to decide to chain me here."

The bench was big enough for them to both sit on if they got close enough. Eira wanted to be very close to her husband tonight. She put her arms around his arm and hugged it tight. They sat quietly for a moment; the sun had gone down and there were not many people on the street. Eira put her head on Corin's shoulder and sighed.

"What are we going to do?" Eira finally asked.

"What do you mean?" Corin asked.

"We are stuck in this house," Eira said, Corin turned to her and put a finger to his lips.

"We should switch to our tongue," Corin said, making the switch himself. "These walls have ears."

"We are here forever," Eira said turning carefully to be able to look at Corin. "What if we have a baby?"

"Then we have a baby," Corin said. "Josephus said something to me the other day, his God says to not worry about tomorrow but to take care of today."

"His God talks?" Eira said, missing the main point of what was said.

"Yes," Corin said, "apparently, he came to walk among his people. Josephus even sat and listened to him talk when he was a boy."

"That would be amazing," Eira said, "Toutatis has left us to die." As she said that a loud noise came from the street. Corin was quickly on his feet, his club in his hand. A Romani in a stained tunic stumbled up to the door. From her place behind Corin, Eira could smell the drink on his breath. Corin blocked the man from getting any closer.

"You're bigger than the last guy," the drink muttered.

"You need to step back," Corin said in a menacing voice.

"We shouldn't have killed him," the drunk said, falling to his knees and weeping.

"Get Josephus," Corin said quietly to Eira. Eira moved quickly into the villa and down the corridor to the slaves' quarters. There were several slaves playing a game on a design they had carved into a bench and some pebbles. Josephus was sitting in the corner with his eyes looking upwards. He seemed to be muttering something. Eira called to him and he stood and walked to her.

"Corin needs you at the entrance," Eira said softly. Josephus nodded and walked down the corridor. Eira wasn't sure if she should follow, but she was very curious. She walked a step behind as was proper and when they came to the door she hid in the shadows.

The drunk man was now sitting on the bench with Corin standing over him. It looked like he had vomited some of his drink, maybe now he would be able to make sense.

"What is all this?" Josephus asked sternly.

"This man says he helped kill the old ostiarius," Corin responded. Eira gasped, she had liked Prisca, he always greeted her with a smile.

"I didn't want to," the drunk cried out, "we were supposed to grab the girl, I'm not a murderer." Josephus looked at the man and put his hand to his chin. He seemed to be looking for a beard to pull at, but no slave was allowed to wear a beard. He then turned to where Eira was standing.

"Girl," Josephus said to Eira, "you should be with Druscilla. However, I need to find more out from this man, go first to get Domine Marcus Fabius." Eira nodded and rushed to the cubicula the Domine shared with the Domina. She was one of the few slaves allowed to wake them, so she knocked on the door without worrying about what they might think.

"Domine," Eira called out, "you are needed at the entrance." The door swung open and he came out, pulling on his tunic.

"What is it girl?" the Domine asked.

"I don't know," Eira said, "I was just passing by and Josephus said to fetch you." Eira had lied because she did not have permission to sit with her husband. The Domine rushed through the atrium to the entryway. Eira really wanted to follow but was afraid he would get angry at her for spying. Eira slowly went back to Druscilla's cubicula where she undressed and got into bed. She lay there wondering what was happening with Corin.

# Chapter 13

Corin woke up with the sun, it had been a late night, but he was responsible for unlocking the door so the kitchen slaves could go to the market. As he watched them leave, he sat on the bench and laid his head on the wall. He didn't dare close his eyes, but he could at least rest his head.

The day before had been a long one. He had been married, laid with his wife and then dealt with the drunk until late in the night. He could have done without the last part. The Domine had asked him to drag the man into the atrium and lock the door. The Domine asked the man who ordered them the take the girl. The drunk wouldn't answer, he just kept saying he didn't want to kill anyone.

The Domine had threatened to have him beaten, he even pointed to Corin, whose size seemed to frighten the man. He still wouldn't say who was behind the kidnapping attempt but said they were going to try again. Without giving any names, he said they were enemies of a senator and objected to the wedding. Corin knew that the daughter was promised but didn't really know anything about a senator.

After some time Domine told Corin to fetch his club, Corin rushed to get his club. When he returned the drunk man was on his knees pleading with the Domine. He did not want to be beaten but he was certain if he told who was behind the kidnapping he would be killed. To placate the Domine, the drunk man said more men would be coming soon to finish what they had failed to do. After another hour of the man repeating the same thing repeatedly, the Domine told Corin to throw the man into the street. Corin dragged the man to the street and threw him bodily onto the cobble stones. The man fled from the domus and the Domine came and sat on the ostarious bench. Corin and Josephus stood waiting for him to speak.

"What are we to do?" the Domine asked. Neither slave was going to answer, only an impertinent slave would answer such a question. After a moment of silence, he turned to them and said, "I would like to know what you think."

"I don't know," Josephus said.

"I will guard this door until my dying breath," Corin said. Not because he felt a closeness to Druscilla, but because any danger to her was a danger to Eira.

"We can get more men," the Domine said to Jospehus.

"They can also get more men," Josephus said.

"He's right," Corin said, encouraged by Josephus' candor. "Roma is full of strong men. Men stronger than me."

"She would be safer away from Roma," the Domine said softly.

"That is wise," Josephus said, "but where?"

"The villa," the Domine said almost to himself, "but it is only an hour walk. That is too close."

"Brittania," Corin said softly. He was thinking of the farthest place from Roma. The Domine let out a laugh.

"Can you imagine my wife living among the barbarians?" the Domine said, he saw Corin's face fall and added "it is good, but maybe too far." The three men stood there quietly for a while before the Domine stood, "I have kept you too long. I will ask the senator."

After the Domine left, Josephus and Corin went to their own places to sleep. Corin made sure the door was locked and slept lightly, waking at every noise. With the morning, he was tired but knew he needed to be on constant guard.

The Domine was out the door earlier than normal. He walked out quickly, checking to make sure Corin was on watch as he walked by. Corin stood as he was walking by, taking the stance of a warrior. The Domine nodded with his approval and rushed off.

A short time later Druscilla and Eira came to the entrance. They looked as if they were about to leave. Corin stopped them and asked where they were going.

"To the market," Druscilla said happily, "I have a sestertius from my mother." The girl proudly held up a coing.

"I'm afraid I can't let you leave," Corin said, looking to Eira for help. While Eira didn't know what was going on, she knew she could trust Corin.

"Of course you can," Druscilla said, "I have permission from my mother." Druscilla stepped out and Corin blocked her path.

"Druscilla," Eira said, "I'm sure Corin has a reason."

"I am going to go out!" Druscilla started to yell. Eira tried to shush her, but the Domina had heard and rushed over to see why her daughter was making a scene. As soon as she saw her mother Druscilla stomped her foot and said, "mother he will not let me go out!"

"Is this true?" the Domina asked.

"I'm sorry," Corin said, "I don't think it is wise for her go alone."

"I suppose you want an excuse to go somewhere with your wife?" the Domina said, "maybe I shouldn't have been so kind to you." The Domina was getting loud as well, and the whole domus could hear her. Fortunately for Corin, Josephus stepped into the atrium to help.

"Domina," Josephus said, "may I speak with you?"

"Of course," the Domina said, "I want to tell you how to put this slave in his place!" Josephus took the Domina aside and started to talk to her quietly. Eira glanced at Corin who was red in the face. He looked tired but was obviously determined to keep Druscilla home. As Josephus spoke, the Domina gasped and then turned back to the others.

"Druscilla you will stay home!" the Domina announced before walking away. Druscilla looked crestfallen and Eira looked unsure of what to do. The child had been waiting for this day for a while.

"Has Eira, I mean Ennia, told you that I killed a wolf?" Corin asked. Druscilla's face lit up. Eira gave Corin a thankful look as he suggested she sit on the bench while he told her the story. Druscilla was entranced by the story of how Corin had tracked down the wolf that had attacked her father's sheep.

"It started when I found the sheep dead in the bushes, obviously killed by a wolf." Corin started, "I found a footprint in the mud nearby and followed the direction it was going. After a while I found another one and saw some broken branches that had wolf fur tangled in it." Druscilla was entranced by the story and sat there hanging off his every word.

"When I got to river," Corin said, "I could see that the wolf was drinking. I lay down in the tall grass and moved, inch by inch closer to him."

"On your belly?" Druscilla asked.

"Yes, on my belly," Corin said, "like a snake, I got so close I could smell him." Corin put his fingers on his nose, pinching it. "He smelled terrible." Druscilla and Eira giggled at the thought. Corin crouched down, as if he was behind the wolf in the story. "I stood up slowly," Corin demonstrated the slow stand, almost imperceptible movement. "And wham!' Druscilla jumped at the exclamation, "I hit it in the head with my club."

"Did that kill it?" Druscilla asked.

"It only made it angry," Corin said, making a funny face. "It turned to attack me, and when it jumped, I threw it down into the water." Druscilla clapped in delight. "It came out of the water and I grabbed it by the neck and wrung it's neck!" Druscilla cheered. Eira gave him a look, he obviously had exaggerated the story, but Druscilla had forgotten her disappointment. With the story was done, Druscilla announced that she was hungry, so Eira took her back in for some food.

"Thank you Corin," Eira said as she escorted the girl back towards safety. Corin had enjoyed the way the young girl hung on his every word. He stayed standing to be alert, he was determined she would stay safe.

When the Domine returned he had two legionaries with him. Corin had not had many positive experiences with these Romani warriors and wasn't happy with them being here.

"This is Gaius and Publius," the Domine said, indicating the two men. "The senator has assigned them to me." With no other explanation than that, the Domine left them at the door and entered his villa. While Corin did not like having legionaries, he realized that he could relax and maybe even close his eyes for a time.

Corin sat on his bench to rest. He was not going to sleep, but his eyes were hurting so he shut them. He was in a state between asleep and awake, aware of everything that was going on around him. He also half dreamed about his old home with his family, watching the sheep and Eira.

As the sun was starting to get lower in the sky the Domine came out to check on the guards. He spoke quietly with the Legionaries, as they spoke two more men came and took their place. A watch rotation had obviously been set; men would be on guard all night. The Domine came over to Corin.

"When you lock the door," the Domine said, "I want you to sleep by Druscilla's door. The legionaries will guard the entrance; you keep my daughter safe." Corin nodded. After the sun set, he moved his small mat to the floor by the girl's cubiculum. As Eira was coming to the cubiculum with the clean clothes that had been drying in the kitchen, she was pleasantly surprised to see Corin there.

"Why are you here?" Eira asked. Corin was surprised that nobody had told her about the threat to Druscilla.

"That man last night said more men are coming," Corin said, "the Domine wants me to guard Druscilla."

"Who's guarding the villa?" Eira asked.

"Two legionaries," Corin answered. Eira let out a low laugh.

"It takes two armed men to replace you," Eira said with a smile. Corin had not seen it that way, but that was a funny thought. Eira took the clothes into the cubiculum and Corin set up his mat across the doorway.

As things quieted down in the house, Corin sat on the floor next to the cubicula. He could hear Eira moving around, he felt like things were improving, he was able to get closer to Eira. It wasn't long before Eira came to the door and joined him on the floor.

"She woke up as I brought the clothes in," Eira said softly, "but she's gone back to sleep."

"I heard you singing to her," Corin said, "you will be a good mother." Eira sighed, she wanted to be a mother, but she didn't want to bring a child into this world of slavery.

"Do you know why men are trying to take Druscilla?" Eira asked to distract herself from that thought.

"They don't want her to marry," Corin said. Eira leaned her head on the wall and looked at the ceiling.

"That makes no sense," Eira said, "she's just a child."

"If she marries the senator's son, the Domine will become more powerful," Corin said. "I don't really know anything about how things work here but parents seem to want their children to marry people who will give them more power." Eira had spent more time with the Domine and Domina than Corin had and knew nothing about their lives outside the domus. It seemed odd that anyone would attack a little girl for political reasons. The Romani way of living was harsh and strange.

Eira and Corin talked late into the night, happy to have a reason to be together. Considering everything going on, it felt wonderful to be together.

# Chapter 14

The next few days they fell into a routine. The Domina finally agreed to let Druscilla to go to the market if the legionaries escorted them. Druscilla walked around like she owned the place. Eira found it amusing to watch the little girl walking a little taller. She had to admit that she loved that little girl.

The rest of the time they stayed in the villa and lived their lives as if nothing was different. Except Corin and Eira spent every evening talking by Druscilla's cubiculum. It was good to get to know each other better. After so many years apart, they had a lot to learn about each other.

During the day Corin would sit with the Legionaries. They were well trained; they would stand on either side of the entryway and keep watch. None of them talked, none of them sat, they just stood there. Corin was impressed by them despite his hatred for what they had done to his village. He had gotten to recognize most of them, but sometimes new men would come.

Corin locked the door every night, and every morning he had to be back in time to open it again. When the guards changed at sunset it was Corin's favorite part of the day because it meant he could lock up and go to Eira. Two new men had come this evening and Corin watched them switch out before locking the door and going to Eira. After a long conversation they decided to get some sleep and Corin kissed Eira before laying down. He was asleep quickly.

Corin was woken by several rough hands grabbing him and pulling him up off the floor. He could feel the cold of a sword pressed against his neck. Whoever was holding him was shorter than he was and was trying to push down to keep control. Corin bent his knees and got his feet under himself and then straightened his legs as fast as he could. His head cracked against the chin of whoever was holding him. The sword came away from his neck as the man holding it cried out.

Corin turned his body and managed to wrench a hand free, he used his free hand to push the sword further away. He realized his legs were still free and he was close to the wall. He put a foot on the wall and pushed with all his might. The man behind him stumbled and fell backwards, Corin falling on top of him. Corin heard the sword clatter on the floor.

One of the other men jumped on top of him, Corin brought a knee up and caught the man in the side, he grunted and fell. Corin tried to get up, but another man jumped onto his back. He wondered how many of them there were as he felt something sharp go into his side. Someone had managed to cut him with their sword.

Enraged by the pain, Corin leapt up, throwing the man. The sword flew away and hit the wall. Corin saw it glisten in light from a lantern. He leapt for the sword and grabbed the hilt just as another hand came down on it. Corin threw a fist blindly but didn't connect with anyone. He wrapped his hand around the hilt of the sword and pulled it away.

Another lantern appeared, Corin didn't know if the men who had attacked were carrying lanterns, but didn't have the time to figure it out. He was now armed and ready for the next person to try to take him on. He swung the sword and connected, hearing the familiar clang of a sword against iron. They had armor.

The pain in his side was increasing. More light was appearing. He saw a flash of red, thrust for the red! A man cried out as the sword sank deep into his flesh. Another man yelled in pain. Where was he? Corin turned to see a familiar figure swinging a sword behind him. It was Eira. Corin didn't take the time to consider how she got a sword, he moved to her side and the two of them fought side by side.

They fought off several more men and Corin could feel his side becoming wet as blood came out of his wound. He could see that Eira was losing strength as she tired. The men kept coming. Corin could see they weren't winning; but they were holding their ground.

Suddenly the corridor was flooded with light as people in the household came running. The noise had alerted them, and they had come prepared for trouble. The Domine had brought his sword and joined the fight. The men that remained all ran. Corin and the Domine chased them from the villa.

As the men ran out the door, Corin collapsed onto the tile floor. The Domine realized he had lost his wolf-man and stopped chasing the intruders. He stood at the door which was swinging on its hinges. Corin wondered how that had happened as he faded into unconsciousness.

# Chapter 15

Corin lay on the bed in the spare cubiculum of the domus. The Domine had called a medicus to tend to his wound. The medicus said he would need to rest and drink a lot of bone broth. He had used thread to sew the wound closed and put honey and olive oil on it. Corin had been here a couple of days and was ready to be up and moving again. The pain was still bad, but he knew he could manage.

Corin shifted on the bed and sat up a little, he lay his arm on the curved part of the wooden structure of the bed to support his body. As he was getting comfortable the door opened and Eira came in with a bowl of broth for him. Fortunately, Eira had avoided being hurt during the attack. Several times he thought back to seeing her there swinging the sword with all her might. She had heard the fight and came to check when a sword landed at her feet. Having never trained with a sword she just started to swing it.

When Corin had first woken the Domine had explained that the legionaries that came to guard the door were in the pay of the people that wanted Druscilla dead. They had broken the lock and come in to kill her in the villa this time. Corin had taken on ten men! Two were dead and another wounded badly.

Now as Corin ate, Eira by his side the Domine came back to his room. He sat in a chair and looked at the two who had saved his daughter. He looked disheveled, he had not slept much the last few nights, having taken Corin's place at Druscilla's door. He was trusting no-one.

"Lupinus," the Domine said, "I owe you my daughter's life." He had said this many times, in the last few days and Corin had learned not to say anything but to just nod. "I have been looking at what I can do, and I think you were right," the Domine put a hand on Corin's arm, "we need to take Druscilla to Brittania."

"Are you certain?" Corin asked.

"Yes," the Domine said, "she will need someone to go with her. Of course, Ennia will need to go, and you are her husband." He left the rest hanging for a minute to let them understand what he was saying.

"We are to return to Brittania together?" Corin asked, a little unsure.

"Yes," the Domine said. "I've bought a place, a caupona in a place called Caerwyn." Corin had never heard of Caerwyn, but if it was in Britannia, it was home. Corin had never heard the word caupona before and gave him a blank stare.

"An inn?" Eira asked, recognizing Corin might not know what it was. "We can stay there?"

"I want you to run it," the Domine said, "if you will. I want to give you something for saving my daughter. I am releasing you from my household, you are now free. I'm hoping you will continue to protect my daughter." Corin and Eira sat silent for a long time. They were free. They could refuse him, but he was offering more. He was offering to take them back to Brittania and a place to live.

"I have cared for Druscilla for many years," Eira said, "I will care for her as long as you need me to."

They needed to move quickly for safety, so Corin suggested they leave before he was completely healed. Eira did not like the idea but recognized the need for a rushed departure. Druscilla was excited about the adventure. The only person who objected was the Domina.

Eira thought it odd, Flavia never spent time with her daughter. Now when the girl was about to go, she was in hysterics. She shouted at Marcus Flavius so loudly that the entire household knew what she thought. Marcus Flavius eventually just told her that it was that or have her life in constant danger. They did not hear her response, but the matter was settled.

They prepared quickly and left in the dark of night. Marcus Flavius had hung dark curtains in the carruca, a closed wagon, so nobody could see inside. The carruca was very comfortable, with many cushions and padded benches. Except for the constant jostling along the cobblestones Corin would be able to rest and heal.

The journey back would go much faster than the journey here. The long road that had been torture on the way to Roma now lay ahead to freedom. After a week on the road, they opened the dark curtains to let in the sunlight. Druscilla had never been this far from her home before and spent the journey asking her father questions.

Every evening, they would stop at an inn on the road and Corin and Eira were encouraged to talk to the people running each inn to learn what they could. Corin was surprised to learn that Eira was able to understand the markings they used to write down information. After the first stop the days in the carruca were spent with Eira and Druscilla teaching Corin how to read.

Marcus Flavius was amused to see his daughter bonding with these two. He could tell they would take good care of her. Once they reached Gaul they took a ship to Britannia. Corin was getting stronger by the day. When they landed in Britannia, Corin felt that he was stronger than he had ever been. He took a deep breath of freedom.

Caerwyn was a small village another three-day ride from the shore. They rode in an open wagon now, not afraid of being seen. Corin and Eira were surprised how much had changed. Roads had been built to make travel faster and villas similar to those in Roma had been built in some areas.

Still, it was home, the people dressed and spoke the same. They saw familiar places and roundhouses nestled away from the road. Corin greeted people everywhere they went, enjoying using his old tongue.

The Caerwyn caupona was set on a small hill set back from the road. The first thing they saw was a wall and an arched entryway that had a wooden sign with three spirals meeting in the middle. They went through the arch into a courtyard, on their left was a kitchen with several tables and benches. On the right was a row of doors that let into cubicula for sleeping. In the middle of the courtyard there was a well and at the far end was another wall with an entrance to some stables.

They were given a quick tour of the inn. There were three cubiculae for guests, the man who had run the inn said that he rarely got more than two guests at a time. The fourth door led to a small bathhouse. As they walked through it, Eira noticed it was bigger than the one at the domus in Roma, but Marcus Flavius mentioned it was small. She supposed inns in Roma had big bathhouses.

The kitchen was big, with a big cook fire built close to the courtyard for cooking. In the kitchen they met Hilarus, the slave who did the cooking for all the guests. He was a small Greek man who was balding and a small scar on his right cheek. Off the kitchen was a small room, separated by a cloth curtain. This was the tabiculum, where they kept the money and records. Off to the left of the kitchen was a staircase that led to the innkeeper's residence. There was a large cubiculum at the top of the stairs, and a smaller one off to the left.

The stables at the back had several stalls for horses and a large area for holding chariots and wagons. In the stable they met Rian, the slave who took care of the animals. He was also responsible for the fire that heated the bath. That was kept burning most of the day and only let to go down in the evenings. He was a big man, who obviously used to physical labor. His brown hair was about shoulder length and seemed to be perpetually dirty.

There was a final slave, a woman named Lidia, who had dark hair and features. She was always sullen and didn't speak much when introduced to them by Aelus Rufus, the man who sold the inn to Marcus Flavius.

Eira did not like the fact that the inn used slaves to operate, but it was the only way to do business. The three set up in their new home above the kitchen. The small cubiculum was given to Eira and Corin and the larger one to Druscilla. They were home in Britannia but still felt like they were in Rome.

# Part III

# The Journey to Freedom
# (Two years later)

# Chapter 16

Eira walked down the stairs slowly. Her stomach had grown more than she imagined was possible. She thought back to the moment she first realized she must be with child; she had rejoiced. Corin had swung her around when she told him. Now she was tired of carrying the child inside of her, why did this take so long?

In the kitchen Hilarus was preparing several loaves of bread to go into the oven. His bread was always good, with a firm outside and soft inside. Hilarus was so named by the previous innkeeper, he was always ready to tell a funny story. He smiled at Eira as she walked through the kitchen to the courtyard. While they had decided to keep the slaves working in the inn, Corin and Eira had treated them like family.

In the courtyard Druscilla was helping Corin with fixing one of the tables. She held the leg on while Corin hammered pegs into it. All the tables were getting old, but the new pegs would give them some more stability. Eira thought about how Druscilla changed over the last two years. When they had moved here, she was a spoiled child, and now she was becoming a thoughtful young woman. Without a slave at her constant disposal, she had learned to do things for herself.

Druscilla had learned to speak the Briton tongue like a native. She would often barter with the traders, making as good a deal as Corin or Eira would have. Sometimes better. She also impressed the Romani visitors. They called her the Domina Parva or "little lady." Eira found that amusing because she always thought of Druscilla's mother when she heard someone say "Domina," this young woman was nothing like the Domina.

Corin was enjoying being the master of this small inn. He treated the slaves well; he even petitioned Marcus Flavius to free Lidia when he learned that she had a husband back in Gaul.

Marcus Flavius had agreed so long as they got a replacement. Corin had found a young girl who was an orphan, begging in the street. She had no family left so they took her in.

"Any sign of your father?" Eira asked as she sat on a bench.

"He should be here any time," Druscilla said, "unless something slowed him down."

Marcus Flavius had sent word a few months back that he was coming. He had not been since he dropped them off and wanted to check on Druscilla and see how business was. They had been steady with people traveling from Londinium to the outer border to trade or on military business.

Even now they had an envoy of the governor staying in one of the rooms. He had a scriba staying with him as well, which meant another room was full. He was visiting the merchants in Caerwyn village to assess taxes.

Taxation was a new concept for Corin. He found it odd to be asked to pay the government for the privilege of living on land the government had taken. Eira did a majority of the dealings with the tax assessor, she was really the most gracious in dealing with all Romani.

The table was ready and Corin climbed up on top of it to test its strength. Druscilla laughed while Eira sighed. It did not matter how old men got, they were always boys at heart.

"That's a strong table," came a deep voice from behind Eira, she jumped up as Druscilla rushed past her.

"Papa!" Druscilla cried, throwing her arms around Marcus Flavius. He laughed and kissed the top of his daughter's head.

"You've grown taller," Marcus Flavius said holding her at an arm's length to look at her, "and you are becoming a woman." Eira had to agree she had developed some womanly curves. Flavius turned to Eira and let out a loud exclamation. "And you are to have a child!"

"Yes," Corin said, "we will have our own child here." Corin called for a man to help carry Marcus's belongings from the wagon. He went out and saw Jospehus, his old friend organizing the luggage.

"Josephus!" Corin exclaimed, "it is good to see you." The two men embraced as Eira came out to see what was going on. Josephus saw her and shook his head in amusement.

"The Lord has blessed you with a child!" Josephus said going to Eira and lightly touching her belly. "May he be a wise child, and may he grow to be strong."

Eira smiled and said, "thank you. It is so good to see you." Josephus went back to managing the luggage. Eira went back to the courtyard and joined Druscilla who was organizing food for her father, who was watching with an expression of amused pride.

"I never thought I would see her like this," Marcus Flavius said to Eira. "She has become a confident young woman. Look at her."

"She has been a big help in running your caupona," Eira said. Druscilla called her father to a table where she was setting out fresh bread and various meat dishes. As he sat on the bench Marcus Flavius invited Eira and Corin to join him.

Once they were sitting comfortably Marcus Flavius pulled out a package from his cloak. He opened it and placed its contents on the table. There were several sheets of papyrus that had official seals on them and a purse of coins.

"We left in such a hurry two years ago," Marcus Flavius started, "I wasn't able to do things properly. I have your paperwork here granting you freedom." He handed a papyrus to each of them with an official seal and a declaration with their names on it, giving them freedom. "These are your certificates of citizenship to Roma," Marcus said handing them other documents. This had their Romani names, Ennia and Lupinus.

"We are citizens?" Corin asked softly. He wasn't sure what to think about that. He was grateful to have official documents though. The Romani's loved to see paperwork to prove you were official. Now he had something to show anyone who asked. He just wasn't sure about how it would look to the people of Brittania if he walked around with a Romani citizenship.

"Yes," Marcus Flavius said with a smile, "our laws allow you to be granted citizenship if you are freed by a magistrate." Eira took the documents and read them, even though Corin had learned to read, she was still better at understanding the words. She smiled when she saw the Romani names on the documents.

"I am now Ennia Flavia Sabinus," Eira said with a giggle. "Does this mean our child will be a citizen as well?"

"Of course!" Marcus Flavius said spreading his arms wide. "When the child is born take him to the governor with this paperwork and he will give them citizenship." Eria gave Corin a look. They had gone from slave to citizens of the most powerful nation in the world. She wasn't sure what to think but was glad she was able to give her child a chance for a good life.

# Chapter 17

Marcus Flavius gave them high praise as he toured the inn and spoke with the government official that had been staying there. The official had told Marcus that the caupana was run with Romani efficiency. The stable at the inn was always kept clean and the animals were treated well. Marcus couldn't find any issue to be concerned about.

One evening after Druscilla and Eira had gone to their rooms for the evening, Marcus pulled Corin aside. They sat at the table with some ale, to discuss the future.

"The people that are trying to stop the marriage between Druscilla and Titus are very powerful," Marcus told Corin. "Apparently another senator who doesn't like me wants his daughter to marry the boy."

"They would kill a girl to get their way?" Corin was a little surprised by that.

"Politics in Roma can get dangerous," Marcus said.

"Why do they hate you so much?" Corin asked.

"If Druscilla marries Titus, then that senator and I will be connected by blood," Marcus explained. This did make sense to Corin, marriage arrangements worked the same way in Britannia.

"Of course," Corin said, "then you will have more power in Roma."

"Which could be good for my family," Marcus leaned back and finished his cup of ale, "and your family as well. The senators influence the appointment of the governors. We could get a governor that will work for the people here." Corin wondered about that, does it really help the people to have a foreign person ruling over them?

He thought about the roads and the new buildings, those made life easier for the people. He also thought about the taxes and the need to register with the government. That made life difficult. Would a different governor make any difference? He wasn't sure.

"We will care for Druscilla as long as needed," Corin said, "she has been a big help in running the caupona."

"I've seen that," Marcus said looking around at the courtyard, "she will be a good wife to Titus. That young man will be good for her as well. He has been strong through all this, telling everyone that he intends to keep his word to marry Druscilla. He has even officially made statements against the other senator for trying to kill his betrothed."

"That is good," Corin said. "I will be sad when she leaves to marry, but I'm sure you and the Domina will be happy to have her in Roma again."

The men continued to talk as a loud scream came from Eira. Corin and Marcus jumped up and rushed to the upper room Corin and Eira shared. Eira was crying out in pain. Corin rushed down the stairs where the orphan girl, Elen, was standing looking scared.

"Elen," Corin called to the girl, "fetch Brynwen." Brynwen was an older woman in Caerwyn who helped women give birth. Elen's eyes lit up as she rushed out of the cauperna toward the village. Corin went back to the room where Druscilla had joined Eira.

"You men can leave," Druscilla said with a smile, "I'll stay with her until the obstetrix arrives." Corin knew that an obstetrix helped Romani women with childbirth. His child would be born in the Britannic way, even if he was to be a citizen of Roma. Brynwen had been delivering babies here longer than Romani invaders have been here.

The men walked to the courtyard to sit with the other men who had heard the commotion and wanted to see what was going on. After what seemed like forever, Elen and Brynwen rushed through the courtyard and up the stairs. The old woman didn't even acknowledge the men sitting there waiting.

They waited for a long time, watching Druscilla and Elen run various errands for Brynwen. Finally, the old woman came down the stairs and walked over to Corin.

"It was a false labor," the old woman said, "her body is preparing, but it will be some time yet." Corin's face fell as he learned he would not meet his child yet. "You can go to her now." Corin rushed up the stairs as the other men went to their own beds.

# Chapter 18

Druscilla had spent the last few days with her father spending as much time with him as she could. When he left, she was sad but went back to work to help the guests with the same energy she had before. She was nothing if not resilient.

A few days after Marcus Flavius left, a new traveler came to the inn. His name was Gaius Valerius Severus, he arrived in the late afternoon with several legionaries. He wore the uniform and army of a general, a red cloak fastened at his right shoulder with a bronze clasp. The clasp matched the bronze armor and helmet, which was decorated with a red crest. They had many generals and other officers stayed with them, but this one stood out. Likely because he stood taller than Corin.

"I'm just here for one night," he announced to Corin, "feed my horses well, they have a long journey ahead." Corin told Elen to feed the horses barely grain. He would charge extra for it. The general also had a girl that served him, a slave. She carried his belongings to his room while the giant man sat at a table and demanded ale. Hilarus brought out the ale and Gaius Valerius grabbed his arm.

"You are from Hispania?" Gaius Valerius asked loudly.

"Yes," Hilarus said softly.

"Good," Gaius said loudly, "I want honeyed pork with garum! I believe that is your national dish. Yes?"

"Well," Hilarus said thoughtfully, "we quite enjoy pork with garum. Your taste is as elegant as your clothes."

"Exactly!" the General said, "I have taste! None of my legionaries think so. Of course, they have not travelled as much as me. The empire is ours to travel and experience!"

"Let me prepare you our best," Hilarus said as he rushed off. Druscilla took his place, keeping the general's cup full.

"You're from Roma?" the General asked her.

"I am Druscilla Flavia," she told him, "my father owns the caupona. I oversee the management." The general laughed at this.

"Your father is a wise man not to trust running his business to these barbarians," Gaius Valerius said.

"Lupinus Flavia is my brother," Druscilla said with a sideways glance at Corin. The general looked at Corin with surprise.

"Of course," Gaius Valerius said. "Nice to be in a place run by good Romani people." Corin finished helping to oversee the general's things before joining him at the table. Gaius slapped his back as he sat.

"Your horse is stabled now," Corin said, "he was hungry."

"He does eat well," Gaius said, "it is good to be in such a place. It reminds me of home. I shall sleep well tonight."

"You are gracious," Corin said.

"I was telling him that our father owns the place," Druscilla said. Corin nodded in understanding, they had used this ruse before to make Romani guests feel more comfortable.

"So why are you in Britannia?" Corin asked.

"There is a group of barbarians who are attacking our forts on the frontier," Gaius said, "I have led the major attacks against all forces that have given us difficulty since the campaign in Britannia began." Corin's eyes narrowed as he wondered.

"Did you ever go to a village named Caerith?" Corin asked with suspicion.

"I never worry about their barbarian names," the General said. Corin wondered if this was the man that led the attack against his home. They had made things difficult for the Romani army but were they enough of a problem for them to call in this man who prided himself in killing "barbarians."

"I had a slave from that village," Corin lied, "taught me the tongue of these people. It has given me an advantage in working here." Druscilla gave him a smile and quickly walked to the kitchen. The General watched her walk away.

"Why is she here and not looking to marry in Roma?" Gaius asked.

"She is betrothed," Corin responded, "but her betrothed is preparing for her, and she wanted a final adventure before settling down."

"She is a beautiful girl," Gaius said, "her future husband is fortunate." Corin looked at Druscilla as she carried a tray of food over to the table. She was becoming beautiful; he had first seen her when she was just a child and in his mind, she was still that child.

"I suppose she is," Corin answered. Druscilla put the tray of food on the table and invited the men to eat before disappearing up the stairs to her room. Corin and his guest ate the honeyed ham, it wasn't a favorite of Corin, but he could eat it. Eira could not stomach the garum sauce since becoming pregnant.

After eating the general left to get some rest and Corin started cleaning up. Hilarus and Elen joined him and the three had everything cleaned up quickly. Corin thought about the fees he would charge this man. The expensive grain, the valuable pork and garum sauce that he had asked for, the quality ale and wine. He would make sure this man paid.

# Chapter 19

"When will this baby arrive?" Eira asked as she tried to get out of bed. "I can't grow any bigger!" Corin laughed as he helped Eira out of bed. Eira quickly put on her cloak, the air was getting cold as the winter season was coming. Corin dressed and headed out to the courtyard. There was a light dew on the ground, Corin shivered a little as he walked to the stable. Elen was feeding the horses from a group of traders that were leaving later in the morning. She was still only thirteen or fourteen years old but had strength that equaled some men. Corin looked at her as she filled one of the grain buckets, she wasn't going to be the most beautiful girl, but she was kind.

"Once you've cared for them," Corin said, "head to the kitchen for some food and to warm up." Elen nodded and put the grain in the trough for the horses before taking two buckets to the well. It took her three trips to get enough water for the horses. Afterward she rushed off to join Hilarus and Eira in the kitchen.

Corin walked through the stable to check on the empty stalls to make sure they were clean enough for any upcoming guests. As he entered one stall, he noticed that there was a stack of hay in a corner where it didn't belong. Corin sighed, Rian was supposed to take care of cleaning the stables and had missed something. He was normally not one to leave a mess.

Corin grabbed a fork to move the hay back to the end where it belonged. As he thrust the fork he hit something solid and heard a soft grunt. Corin pulled back and moved the hay with his foot. It suddenly exploded and a man jumped out.

The man had looked like his face had melted, it was obvious he had been badly burned in the past. The tunic he was wearing was torn and very dirty. Corin stepped back and pointed his fork at the man in a defensive stance. The man stepped back as well, but he was against a wall and had no path of escape. The man crouched down, ready to fight when he suddenly stood up.

"Corin?" the man asked. Corin stayed in his defensive stance.

"How do you know my name?" Corin asked.

"It's me, Bran," the man said. Corin inched forward and turned his head. He could see it in the man's eyes, it was Eira's brother, Bran. Corin dropped the fork and embraced his old friend.

"Bran!" Corin exclaimed, "you're alive! Come we need to let Eira know."

"Eira's alive?" Bran asked.

"Yes!" Corin led Bran through the stable to the kitchen. Eira was standing by the fire to warm up, when Bran saw her he called out her name. Eira recognized her brother's voice before she saw him and turned quickly. Her face fell when she saw him, he was not easy to recognize with his face covered in scars.

"Bran?" Eira asked quietly, "is that really you?" Bran stepped forward and took his sister's hand.

"It is," the two embraced in tears. After a minute they separated and Bran held her at an arm's length to look at her. "Look at you," Bran said, "all grown up and expecting a child!"

"How did you escape?" Eira asked, "did father escape? Who else is alive?" Eira led Bran to a bench by the fire to sit.

"I was badly burned with the Romani burned down the village," Bran stated, "I managed to get to the river and travelled to our house where I was able to hide. Seren found me there and nursed me to health."

"Seren?" Eira asked.

"Yes she comes from Pen-Mor," Bran explained. Pen-Mor was a village a few days' walk from theirs. There were often fights between the two villages; they had been raised to distrust anyone from Pen-Mor. "She had seen the smoke while foraging in the woods and came to investigate. She saw a trail and followed it to our house.”

“Nobody else survived?” Eira asked.

“I didn’t think so,” Bran said, “but here you are. Maybe others survived. How did you escape?” Eira spent the next few minutes explaining the brave actions of Corin, being captured, living in slavery and finally being given freedom. As she shared the story, Corin joined them and added some of his own details. “That is some story,” Bran said as they finished.

“What have you been doing?” Corin asked.

“I’ve been working with the resistance,” Bran said, “we have been keeping them from moving further towards the hills, but we have lost ground. I managed to escape, but a few days ago they captured many of our warriors and crucified them.” Corin was familiar with crucifixion as it was a popular punishment for anyone that defied Romanic rule.

“I’m not sure you would be safe here,” Eira said, “we have Romani guests all the time.”

“You allow them to sleep under your roof?” Bran asked, incredulously.

“I let them give me their money,” Corin responded.

“Bran,” Eira said softly, “some of them have become friends.” This obviously upset bran. “We have gotten to know them, and some are not bad people.”

“Not bad people?” Bran stood up and slammed his fist on the table, “they have come here to destroy our way of living!” As he was talking, Corin saw Druscilla walking down the stairs. She was still looking a little tired but obviously was curious what all the yelling was about.

“Bran,” Corin said, standing and putting a hand on Bran’s shoulder, “please, we don’t want to upset you. We have had an experience living in their country, you must understand…” Corin could not finish as Bran shoved his hand away and rushed out into the courtyard. He turned and pointed at Corin.

"You used to be a great warrior" Bran shouted, "but you are just a Romani slave." Bran held his right arm straight in front of himself in a mockery of the Romani salute, "ave!" Bran shouted as he stormed out of the cauperna. Eira stood to go after him, but Corin held her back.

"Let him calm down," Corin said, "he has a right to be upset." Eira sat again but the tears running down her face showed she did not want to let Bran go. Corin sat beside her and held her.

"Who was that?" Druscilla asked as she came into the kitchen.

"My brother," Eira said softly.

"I didn't know you had a brother," Druscilla said, sitting beside Eira.

"We thought he was dead," Eira explained, "killed when our village was burned down." Druscilla was taken aback by this statement. She had never really learned what had led to her favorite people joining her household.

Druscilla understood that slaves were taken from their home and brought to Roma. Growing up she had been taught that the places they left were barbaric and people lived hard lives. It was better for them in Roma with bathhouses, good food, and civilized people. The idea that they might have lost everything had never occurred to her. She knew Corin and Eira as two wonderful people, not just barbaric slaves.

Druscilla then realized that the "barbarians" were the people of Britannia. She knew these people and they were not barbarians. Maybe their houses were different, and they had some different way, but sometimes their way made more sense.

"Your village was burned down?" Druscilla asked.

"Yes," Corin said matter of fact, "when the Romani army came, they burned our village to the ground, took us from our home, marched us to Roma and humiliated us in front of everyone in the marketplace. Eira was no older than you are now." Druscilla's face fell. She thought back to visiting the market and seeing the slaves on display. She never thought of the humiliation it might bring them. She started to cry and looked up at Eira.

"You must hate all of us!" Druscilla said. Corin felt bad for how harshly he had spoken. Of course he didn't hate Druscilla, and he knew Eira adored her. He crouched down to where she was sitting and looked her in the eye.

"I don't hate you," Corin said. Eira put an arm around Druscilla.

"I don't either," Eira said.

"You were just a child," Corin said calmly, "you can't be blamed for what your parents did. You are a good person." Druscilla gave him a sad smile.

"Really?" she asked.

"Of course," Eira said, pulling Druscilla around so she could look her in the eye. "I hated your father for what he did, buying me like a piece of meat. When I met you, I realized what was needed. You needed someone to care for you."

"I did?" Druscilla sniffed as she spoke.

"Do you remember what you first said to me?" Eira asked.

"Not really," Druscilla responded.

"You said my ears were like the handles of a jug," Eira said. Druscilla and Corin laughed.

"Your ears were big," Druscilla said.

"They were!" Corin added, laughing "you described them well." Eira slapped Corin playfully.

"Corin!" Eira said.

"I thought it was cute," Corin smiled at his wife as he stood up. "You're beautiful now." He kissed her on the forehead.

"What I want to say," Eria said blushing, "is that our opinions of people change over time. You didn't like me at first and I don't like you. When we got to know each other, we became good friends." Druscilla sighed and stood up.

"We are good friends," Druscilla said. She walked over to the kitchen where Hilarus was preparing food and joined him in his work. They might still have slaves, but she decided it was important to treat them well.

# Chapter 20

Corin could smell the snow in the air, he couldn't describe what that meant other than he knew snow was coming. He loved how the blanket of white changed the landscape. Corin walked up the small path that led to the village of Caerwyn, he could have walked the road, but this path was quiet and had a better view of the fields.

Corin pulled his cloak tighter and looked across the field to a group of roundhouses sitting in a shallow valley. He thought back to living in the cozy house, sitting around the fire and listening to his father tell stories from their family. He missed his family on days like this, wishing that his mother would still be waiting with a bowl of warm potage and a cup of ale.

As he walked on towards the village, he spotted a person sitting on a fallen log by the trail. As he got closer, he recognized the scarred face of Bran. He had received a message from Bran earlier that he wanted to talk without Eira around. Corin had sent a message back to meet on this path.

"Corin," Bran said, standing as Corin approached. "Thank you for coming."

"Eira wants you to know you are welcome to come back," Corin said.

"I don't think it would be safe," Bran said. Corin nodded, he was right, they had many Romani staying there. That loud general Gaius was at the inn again talking all about putting down the barbarians that were causing problems. Eira tried to like all people, but she confessed to Corin at night that she could not stand that man.

"Likely not," Corin said. The two men sat on the log and stared out across the valley. The air was getting colder and they both pulled their cloaks tight.

"I want to talk to you about the resistance," Bran started, "I know you work for the Romani now, but do you have any devotion to the old ways?" Corin was a little offended by the question. He had embraced Romani life, little by little, because it made sense. He had to live like them to survive, and now he was doing more than surviving. He was able to do anything he wanted for his wife and future children.

He also wanted to teach his children about their ancestors. He wanted his son to experience taking the sheep out on a summer morning and watching them graze across the hillside. He wanted his daughter to work with her mother to collect firewood to make the home warm and comfortable. He especially wanted to sit by the fire and tell the stories of his ancestors.

"I do," Corin finally said. "However, I have been given something special. I am a citizen of Roma; they have given me freedom."

"At what cost?" Bran asked softly, "the enslavement of your brothers?" Corin had not thought of that at all. He had slaves in his inn; two he had inherited and one he had added. None of them were treated like slaves, but they also could not leave. He had put Elen in that position himself by bringing her in.

"We have always kept slaves from other villages," Corin said defensively. Bran turned to him with a look of incredulity.

"Slaves?" Bran spat out, "I don't care about slaves! It is worse than that! We never took land and forced everyone on the land to pay us!" Corin thought about that, it was true that the Romani had done more than just take a few slaves. They had made everyone their slaves by forming a government and forcing them to pay taxes. The Britons had never had anything like that.

"What am I to do?" Corin asked. "I'm one man."

"A man with a powerful advantage," Bran said. "You have Romani government and military speaking openly around you. If you join the resistance, you can bring us information."

Corin thought about that, it was tempting to help his fellow Britons with information. It was also dangerous. He was a Roman citizen now and wasn't sure how they would respond if he was caught. The Romani government were often cruel to anyone they felt was against them.

He also had responsibilities that Bran didn't have. He had Eira and his unborn child. He couldn't put them in danger. He also had Druscilla to think about. If he was caught as a spy, would the Romani government see her as an innocent caught up in it all?

"I'm not sure," Corin said, "I need to think of the safety of my family."

"This is bigger than your family!" Bran exclaimed, standing and looking down at Corin. "This is the land of our people!"

"Yes!" Corin stood, towering over Bran, "but the people need to stay alive for it to stay that way. The people of that small village where Londinium stands didn't fight and they are all alive. Working with the Romani they have become the most powerful people in Britannia."

"That makes no sense," Bran stepped closer, he would not back down "They may think they are powerful, but they are not free to do what they want!"

"They have accepted their place," Corin said, "as have I, we lost to the Romani in Caerith because they are much stronger than we are. I have influence among the strong now. I will not be a part of the weaker force again." Bran stood there glaring at Corin. He had hoped Corin would see his side but realized now he had been Romanized.

Bran turned and walked off. Corin had hoped this conversation would go better, for Eira's sake. She wanted to be able to sit with her brother again like the old days. He hated to see Bran go, he also hated to think he was betraying his people, but he needed to protect his family.

As Corin arrived back at the inn, it was full of activity. Hilarus took Corin's arm and pulled him into the kitchen.

"Brynwen is here," Hilarus said, "Eira's water came." Corin wanted to rush to his wife's side but knew that would not be allowed. Birthing babies was a woman's domain and men were not welcome. Corin sat on the bench as Hilarus brought him a cup of ale.

The day dragged on and soon the snow was falling. The courtyard was quickly covered with a blanket of white. Corin watched as guests arrived and Hilarus and Rian took care of them. They were traders traveling, but Corin did not care to talk to them. All he could think about was his wife.

As the sun set, Hilarus put some food on the table for guests and Corin just sat and stared into the fire they had built in the courtyard to keep things warm. Snow was still falling and the world seemed quiet. He expected to hear screaming from Eira, but there was nothing.

As he got tired, Corin pulled his cloak around himself and lay down by the fire to sleep. He had slept this way many times before as a shepherd. He slept fitfully, starting at every noise, hoping for news. Finally as the sun came over the horizon, Druscilla shook him awake. She was smiling and helped him to his feet. Without a word she took him by the hand and led him to the room. There on his bed lay Eira, she looked tired but happy. In her arms was a small bundle. Their child.

"Come meet our son," Eira said smiling. Corin stepped forward and looked down at the small child sleeping. "I want to call him Aedan," Eira said.

"Little Aedan," Corin said. "He's perfect, and you are amazing!" Corin kissed his wife. As he stood there looking at this boy he was stuck with an incredible sense of love and duty. He would do anything for this child. Anything to protect his future!

Coming in soon from
D.W. Lewis

# Freedom

Book II of the Caerwyn Chronicles

The following is a preview of *Freedom*"...

Aedan walked through the busy streets of Londinium, the air was thick with the smell of humanity. He had been here many times before with his parents, but this was his first time coming alone.  He wasn't totally alone, Rian, the slave from the inn was with him. Rian preferred to stay with the wagon and the mules, so Aedan was practically on his own. He was there to buy supplies needed for the family run caupona; most of their guests were Roman or Roman supporters who wanted Roman food.

The columns that formed the front of the marketplace towered over Aedan as he walked past. The courtyard that he walked into was busier than the streets if that were possible. There were people dressed in Romani fashions and people dressed in the old way, true Briton fashion. Of course, there was a constant reminder of who was in power, the legionaries who marched through the market.

The food stalls that sold Romani food were all in a certain section of the market. Aedan hated the path over there because he needed to walk past the slave market. It was a small section of the market, but visible. The Romans liked to remind people that they could control their lives even more if they didn't behave. Aedan made it a point to avert his eyes ever since he was a child. The humiliation the people went through was more than he liked to see.

As he was walking past, something caught his eye. There was a flash of color he didn't expect and he turned without thinking. On the platform was a girl with hair the color of glowing embers. He had never seen anything like that before. She had a strong jawline and a short nose. She was standing on the platform, trying to cover herself. They had just removed her tunic, and she stood there wearing only a loincloth. She wasn't crying or complaining, she glared at all the men there as if daring one to come too close.

Aedan remembered his mother's stories of experiencing a similar humiliation when she was sold as a slave. His temper flared, he stepped into the throng of people at the market he could hear some of the men saying crude things he would not dare repeat. They were talking about that girl with ember-colored hair. Aedan felt the anger inside of him rising. The man on the platform raised his hand for silence.

"This young barbarian comes from the far north, beyond the northern border. She would be a good addition to your household." The men started to talk again, more comments that disturbed Aedan. "We can start with eight hundred sestertii," the man continued.

"Here," said one of the men. Aedan did not like the way he looked at the girl. He looked at his purse and thought about the two thousand sestertii he had scraped together for this trip. It represented three months of caring for guests, three months of hard work for his parents, himself and his brother and sister. Aedan did most of the calculations for the inn, he knew what the money was worth.

"Is there an increase on eight hundred?" the man on the platform was saying. Aedan raised his hand without thinking. "Ah the young man wants her, perhaps he needs companionship." That comment brought jeers and laughter from the other men. Aedan was sick that anyone would think that of him. The decision to bid had been impulsive compared to the way Aedan normally acted. Another bid was made and he was ready to quit. He had no logical reason to save this girl. Slavery was part of life and what happened to the slaves was none of his business.

Aedon sighed and turned to leave. He couldn't responsibly spend any money on this. It was a foolish idea to bid, what if he had won? He would be responsible for a slave and not have enough to buy the supplies needed. As he walked off, he thought about his sister. This girl was about her age; his sister was worth more than two thousand sestertii. Without giving it another thought he turned and bid one thousand!

"He's desperate for companionship," the slave trader called out amidst a round of laughter. "What do you say men?" There was another round of laughter and men calling out obscene suggestions. Another man bid and Aedan decided that maybe the gods had saved him from his own rash actions. He didn't need to be responsible for a slave; he had enough to take care of. As the oldest of three children, he was expected to take care of his siblings and help run the family inn. Aedan turned away again and started to head to the stalls he needed to visit.

"Young man," the slave trader called, trying to increase the bid. "Look at her, such beauty, you can't just walk away, cay you?" This was met by more laughter and jeers. Aedan felt the blood rush to his face and turned back to face the man.

"One thousand, four hundred!" Aedan heard himself saying. He didn't know what compelled him, he just knew that this poor girl deserved better.

"Sold!" the man threw the girl's tunic at her, and she rapidly put it back on.

Aedan slowly walked to the platform and counted out the coins The man roughly pushed the girl to him and laughed. Aedan grabbed the girl's hand gently and led her away from the laughter.

At first the girl resisted, and Aedan wasn't sure why. Then he realized, if she was from the north she likely had not learned any Latin. She was likely Caledonian, Aedan had heard of them but never met one.

"Come with me," Aedan said in his own tongue. It was different from the tongue of the Caledonians, but he knew they were similar enough to communicate. He prayed to the gods that she would understand. She seemed to understand but shook her head. Aedan put his arm around her and whispered that these men wanted to hurt her and he wouldn't allow it. She finally went with him.

When they got to the wagon Rian looked at Aedan and the girl. Rian was in his late forties and hated just about everyone. This oldest son of his master did have some redeeming qualities; he had taken after his mother in appearance and intelligence. His father Corin Lupinus was a big and powerful man, while Aedon was average size and strength. His dark hair was straight, and he always kept it clean and combed. He also kept his jaw clean shaven, although he likely wasn't old enough to grow a beard.

"What is this?" Rian asked.

"I bought this girl," Aedan said. "It was a quick decision that will likely get me into trouble." Rian laughed, he turned to the girl and asked her in the Caledonian tongue what her name was.

"Maeli," the girl said softly. Aedan looked at Rian in disbelief. He had never asked the man where he had come from, he just knew he was from the north.

"Maeli," Rian said, "where are you from?"

"Coire Mór" the girl replied. Rian nodded, he knew the place, it was obvious that his young master did not.

"She's from the far north, the islands," Rian said. "She's a Caledonian."

"What am I to do?" Aedan said. "It took almost all my money to get her away from them." Rian smiled again.

"It seems our young master feels he has made a mistake," Rian said to Maeli. Maeli looked lost, "he's spent the money he was to use for food to give to the slavers. You are beautiful, I can see why he would do that." Maeli just glared at the men while Aedan found himself blushing. She was beautiful, her red hair was tangled but still stood out. She had a softly curving jaw and eyes the color of the sea.

Aedan told Rian and Maeli to get into the wagon, he would have to go home empty handed. They had enough supplies for a few more days; he prayed to the gods that a wealthy visitor would come that he could charge extra. He had done that before, his mother didn't like it, but his father approved. The trip home would take a day, and he could try to think of a way to tell his parents what he had done.

If you would like to learn more about Caerwyn and our author DW Lewis visit our Patreon page.


www.patreon.com/renhands


OR


Visit
www.dwlewisbooks.org/caerwyn-chronicles